MW00916684

THEY BROUGHT TARNISHED SECRETS

SHARON SANANGELO

authorHOUSE®

AuthorHouse™
1663 Liberty Drive
Bloomington, IN 47403
www.authorhouse.com
Phone: 1 (800) 839-8640

Published by AuthorHouse 08/29/2019

ISBN: 978-1-7283-2475-3 (sc)
ISBN: 978-1-7283-2473-9 (hc)
ISBN: 978-1-7283-2474-6 (e)

Library of Congress Control Number: 2019912562

A Sincere Dedication

To my dear friend, Hannelora. You are my inspiration!

CONTENTS

C H A P T E R |

THE TAILOR'S FAMILY

The threat of world war hung heavy in the air, as the steady hands of the tailor cut a pattern in the soft cloth. He had learned his craft by working with a Master Tailor for four years. Anton was both serious and focused during this time. Cobblers and carpenters experienced this same method of becoming a skilled worker. Anton, being the responsible man he was, waited for the day of the tailor test with great patience and some anxiety. He passed and excelled in all areas. Anton felt proud and pleased with himself. For many years these repetitive yet calm motions created a living for his family. Today, there would be an abrupt, raw end to the life they lived together.

Anton referred to a book of careful measurements that his pencil had scratched on paper during his years of sewing. Katica watched her loving husband at work.

At times Anton would pause to gaze through the

window to see the land of Croatia where his German parents had settled. The tailor's mind drifted back to the words of his father and grandfather. Anton, as a young boy, had listened with great interest.

It all began in the year 1865 when the Austrian monarchy sent German people to work and settle the land. They spoke the words of the German language, specifically the Swabian dialect.

By day, Anton's ancestors walked the lush, green fields to herd the thick, woolly-haired sheep. Others were skilled in raising and caring for graceful Lipizzan horses.

The days of their lives passed with peaceful co-existence with the Croatians. Yugoslavian rule held this Baltic state.

Anton's thoughts returned to a meaningful time when his first daughter was born. His love for a farmer's daughter resulted in the lovely girl of five years, who sat beside him. Mirjana's dark, wavy hair and dark eyes mesmerized people who knew her.

Anton's younger daughter, Maria, toddled around their home. At three years of age, Maria's smile often spread across her little, round face.

The calm work of sewing by hand or machine often allowed the tailor's thoughts to wander. He must concentrate despite the ominous feeling of suffocation in his chest.

"Papa, your eyes tell me something is concerning you. You're worried. I know you are," Mirjana asked gently.

"In time, my dear daughter, in time I will talk to you,"

Anton replied. The warm, tender moments between mother, father, and daughters would soon be threatened.

It was only the following day when the command came, like a bolt of lightning from a dark sky. Loud knocks sounded on the thick, heavy door when the courier's strong hand struck the wood.

Katica opened the door feeling like a meek girl instead of the mother she really was. A tall unfamiliar man hurled loud words at her. "Where is the tailor? We know he lives here."

In the back room of their home, Anton had set aside his heavy iron sewing shears. He had heard the unpleasant, unwanted intrusion.

"I'm here, what do you want of me?"

Anton's hard stare was directed at the burly man who darkened the entrance to their humble but pleasant home.

The stranger answered with strict words of authority. "The German military wants you!"

With a strong reply, Anton responded, "I'm not a fighter! I was meant to be a father and a tailor."

Anton's direct look cut through the courier's gray eyes which looked like two, hard stones. In return, the messenger saw the face of a man who held definite beliefs.

The words of this large man who represented the military were shouted at Anton. "They want you to repair German military uniforms. Pack a small bag. You are to come with me."

The year was 1940 – Anton had been recruited by the German military. Intense thoughts of separation and fear flooded through his mind. Anton felt like his head was ready to burst. He could not leave his wife and daughters. His love was too deep. He just could not do it!

The messenger's sneer curled his upper lip as he watched Anton. The invisible scorn between the two men filled the room.

Only minutes later, with his small bag, limp on his arm, Anton walked past his beloved wife and beautiful daughters. Love and sadness passed between their faces – a deep love hovered in the air. And then he was gone....

CHAPTER 2

THE SAD JOURNEY BEGAN

Chaos and confusion rushed through Katica's mind. What had just happened? Sadness slapped her face as the abrupt separation began. Think, think, you must concentrate! The thought echoed back and forth inside her head.

Katica, being the good mother she was, focused on her children. She took Mirjana's hand with great tenderness. "We must get Maria. She is sleeping in her room."

Katica's thoughts swirled as she spoke softly to Mirjana. "At least only one of you watched as your father left us." Mirjana's large, dark eyes looked back at her mother. Mirjana usually knew just the right words to say. This moment, she said nothing.

Katica walked with slow, heavy steps across the room to a well-worn couch, past the faded furniture and into Maria's room. She blinked away hidden tears as she talked to Maria. "Your father had to go away for awhile." Katica stroked Maria's thick black wavy hair as she spoke.

Mother and two daughters sat together in silence as they absorbed what had happened. Katica forced her mind to become calm and organize her thoughts from the sudden sadness of separation to what actions to take now.

She would grow in strength and care for her daughters alone. The word crept inside her being, alone...

Minutes later, Katica's clear thoughts jumped in rapid progression from the cold facts of living alone with her two daughters to the reality of how to do it.

Whispered words haunted Katica's mind. As she walked around the Croatian village, she heard stolen moments of time when the people spoke about their fears. Her Anton had been taken to a foreign country against his will!

Disbelief, shock set in as Katica moved even closer to Mirjana. What could she do to keep them safe?

Katica stared into the empty home around her. She tried to change her tense breaths into a slow, peaceful pattern. Katica had to continue with this severe life change. There was only one thing to do. She would take her daughters and live with her parents. There would be food and some small amount of security.

With only a vague knowledge of what she was doing, Katica packed clothing and some belongings that held meaning for a family beginning a fright-filled stage of their lives. She moved with her mind in a misty haze, almost unaware of what she was doing.

Katica's steps were cautious and heavy as she walked the short distance to her parents' home. She grasped

Maria's hand – the other hand held a small bag of life memories. Mirjana being herself, sometimes impulsive, had raced ahead.

The power of strong love between a mother and two daughters was palpable in the air. The deep silence around them spoke louder than words. Deep within, Katica vowed to protect them from all that would come.

She failed to see the soft green grass and bright blue sky as the three moved closer to her parents' home. Katica's soft knock on the door told of their arrival.

As the heavy wood door opened, one look between the older mother and her daughter was poignant as their eyes met in silence. Katica's mother stretched her arms around her daughter and two granddaughters.

A new life would begin – one of loneliness, separation and suspicion. Suspicion would descend into fear for their future. The specter of the world in war crept into the people's thoughts. Horrors they could not comprehend with deaths born out of evil would soon be upon them.

The days struggled to become tolerable for all. Katica's parents, Hannah and Matej, supported her and their grandchildren, amid their own fears.

As the pale, yellow rays of each morning's sunrise stretched across the lush, green land, Matej, Katica's father, started his daily work. With the work of many hands, the earth gave gifts of bright orange carrots, hearty potatoes, onions, red beets and peppers. Matej and his neighbor Croatians farmed the land. Others butchered the animals they raised to sustain their own lives.

In fields not far, other Croatian men cared for the

Lipizzan horses. On this particular morning Matej had an idea. He spoke to the man hoeing beside him. "I must take my granddaughters to see the horses. Their hearts are heavy and I only see sadness in their young, beautiful eyes." Resting for a moment on his hoe, the man replied, "You should do that, Matej."

A small idea had been born and it would happen even if only moments of joy occurred.

Back in their small home, another idea of larger consequences was lighting the mind of Katica. As Matej had been thinking of his granddaughters, Katica had been remembering her father's eyes that told the true story. His voice could not yet say the words.

There were other words that pounded the air outside their home. Syrians screamed at Croatians as they passed in the streets. Why was there such a strong current of underlying tension? Was fear knifing its way through their minds?

CHAPTER 3

SMALL JOY TO INTENSE FEAR

A new day began with a grandfather's desire to bring joy to his granddaughters. Matej's work in the vegetable fields could wait for a small time.

He turned and took their young, soft hands. "Come girls, let's walk to the stables."

"Oh, Opa, can we, can we go?" Mirjana was always the first to answer with her enthusiasm showing. Her bright, positive ways had been subdued since they arrived.

"Yes, my dears, it is time," Matej responded with a hint of a smile.

The well-kept stables were not far from the fields. Matej's granddaughters scampered ahead of him in excitement.

Within minutes they reached the large barns with open doors to give the prized Lipizzans plenty of fresh air. The girls' eyes widened as they saw stall after stall of pure white horses.

As Mirjana and Maria stepped inside they watched as the Lipizzans' large heads reached into the shiny buckets filled with oats. The girls stared with awe at the magnificent horses.

After a few mouthfuls of their delicious oats, the horses noticed their admirers. Matej slipped his hands into his pockets to retrieve red, polished apples. "Maria, Mirjana, here are apples you can give to the horses for special treats."

Their eager hands grabbed the apples with anticipation of the next several minutes of time. Matej relished the smiles and looks on the girls' faces as they fed the horses. Their long, rough, pink tongues tickled the palms of the girls' hands. Maria and Mirjana looked at each other with smiles and giggles.

"We probably should leave now, girls," Matej sighed. A few precious moments had been added to their uncertain lives.

As they walked back to their home, a sharp contrast presented itself in Matej's mind. The beauty of the Lipizzan stallions was marred by the Turkish soldiers who fought wars on horseback. Much like life, so much good and beauty around us often gets destroyed by clashes in diverse ideology and beliefs.

Enough serious thinking – Matej had to prepare for the future he could not stop!

As the thick clouds and darkness of night crept over the Croatian village, Matej watched as his family prepared for rest of body and mind. The girls were still talking about their vivid experiences with the horses.

The girls' grandmother, Hannah, listened with care as she stirred the thick stew in the black pot made of cast iron. Tonight the family would steal an hour, maybe two hours, of happiness together. The steaming vegetable stew tasted so good as the girls excited words about the stunning white horses warmed them all inside.

Evening came and with it time to settle Mirjana and Maria into their small beds. Katica gently pulled the soft blankets over the girls' shoulders.

Outside the bedroom, Katica glanced through the hallway window. Thin barren black branches seemed to stretch across the bright, white moon. This glowing moon seemed captured by a thick, large spider web. It foreshadowed what would come!

And now the long night of fear began.....

****

The drummer had walked the old stone streets that day. He struck heavy sounds of warning on his worn drum. The villagers understood his ominous message. This could be one of the many nights when the dreaded Partisans came.

Inside the gray, stone church, the village night guards walked and watched. Their eyes peered into the darkness of night.

One of the guards spoke, "Look in the distance. There's slow movement in the overgrown bushes."

Thick branches were disturbed by large, muscular bodies. Again the guard spoke, "It's the Partisans, they're coming."

His legs could not carry him fast enough to get to the heavy, old bell rope. The guard's hands grasped the thick, prickly rope and pulled with all his strength. Chimes rang out from the heavy, metal bell. Its sounds echoed through the village air.

The musical tones of the bells used to calm the people as they called them to pray and worship. Now the sound was an ominous warning.

Katica heard the bells first, jolted out of her small bed and rushed to her daughters. "Maria, Mirjana, wake up, hurry, hurry!"

Mirjana stirred slightly and turned her head on her soft pillow. She whispered, "Mother what, what do you want?"

"Come on, we must get your sister now!" Katica replied. With swift steps, almost stumbling, they came to her bed.

"Maria, you must wake up." Katica gently rubbed her younger daughter's shoulder. Puzzled and confused, Maria finally responded to her mother's persistent touch.

Both girls were dazed but standing. Katica made her way slowly through the house with her arms wrapped around each daughter. In the darkness, she felt her way along the familiar worn furniture. Katica kept her daughters very close until she finally reached the kitchen.

In the heavy darkness of night, they knew with sharp instinct that something was very wrong. Every human sense they possessed snapped into alertness. Their fear was true in vivid detail. Katica attempted to calm her mind, to concentrate on doing the right thing and taking the best action.

Her father, Matej, was already there in the kitchen waiting for them. Concern – no, a fearful pain – spread across his face.

Matej's stern command, "Hannah, help me push the table."

Hannah rushed to help Matej move the heavy, wood table. Katica bent to the floor and forced the faded rug away. In immediate succession, Matej reached for the metal circular hardware almost flush to the floor boards. He pulled slowly upward. The hidden door to the basement was revealed!

Matej had never opened a door with so much purpose in his entire life. With swift but steady movement, he helped his loved ones down the short, rickety steps to the damp, musty basement.

Hannah was the first to descend into the darkness. Mirjana and Maria followed with their small shaky footsteps. As Katica's turn came, her thoughts shot back and forth in her mind. Brutal danger was almost upon them and yet her thoughts went to Anton. Where was he? If only he could have been there with them at this moment.

Katica snapped her thinking back to the frightening scene around her. Her father's legs were steady, deliberate as he joined his family below their usual living space.

Once all their feet touched the dirt floor, he stretched his arm far above to pull the faded rug back across their hiding place.

The small wood door, an old rug and a farm table, a little out of its place, were all silent pieces. They, too, waited to see if their presence offered protection.

Below, the small family breathed short, shallow breaths of fear. Matej knew that some of the other villagers had also made secret doors to secret places. Protection of family was their priority above all.

Deep in the ground, in their musty basements, the frightened people could hear the loud sounds of horror. Katica softly stroked Mirjana's wavy, dark hair sometimes covering her ears to muffle the dark noise. With her other arm, Katica held Maria close. As Katica disguised her own fear she spoke to her girls. "Try not to listen. We are safe here together."

"But I want my father, my Papa. Why did they take him?" Mirjana's words poured out between her sobs.

****

Outside the village, men's heavy footsteps pounded the ground as they herded the livestock from the fields into the barns. The Partisans wanted the animals not only for food, but to strike another level of fear into the villagers.

They were successful in their cruel mission. Fewer animals grazed the once peaceful fields.

The most permanent fear was forever etched deep into the souls of this peaceful village. The sound invoked by the evil actions of the Partisans echoed through the air.

Katica covered her girls' ears and pulled them even

closer. She endured emotional pains as she listened to the screams of the women outside their home.

The brutal, vicious Partisans stole the animals and attacked the women without mercy. Rough hands tore at their clothing. The village women's ripped peasant clothing revealed their soft, fair skin. Tears spilled from their eyes and passed slowly down frightened faces.

Time seemed to stop as the terror continued. She held silent screams in her throat ..... stop, stop!

The end was not near as the front door was pushed in with great force. Katica's words of horror slipped from her lips, "Oh, not here, my daughters are with me."

Heavy footsteps crashed against the bare wooden floor boards. Katica's heart pounded as she looked into her girls' eyes. She placed her fingers to her lips to emphasize they must be silent.

Above them the dreaded men continued their mission of hate. They searched every small room, every corner. One of the men hurled loud words at the other. "What do you think? They must have gone."

The second man's reply cut through the air. "I hate it when some escape. It makes me want to hurt them more and really drive them out."

They lingered a few minutes longer with their cold eyes darting around the rooms. Only a few feet below them, Katica and her family shivered with dreaded anticipation.

"Come, hurry, there are more to find." The Partisans thundered out the door without closing it.

Only moments before, the pace of the heavy footsteps had quickened. The men's attention snapped from this home to other homes where their evil rampage would harm another family.

Matej watched Katica, Mirjana and Maria. Hannah's eyes held them all in her steady stare. The adults' faces focused with strong resolve. They would survive this ordeal.

As the hidden family waited, they could hear the Partisan's pause. Their breaths caught the night air. The sky was filled with bright stars in sharp contrast to the evil ways of these men.

Mirjana and Maria moved slightly under Katica's arms. Their movements brought Katica's thoughts back to their stale hiding place where the dampness of the basement crept into her nose.

The girls' fear changed to restlessness. Katica listened for sounds from outside. The sharp screams had ended. Soft sobs broke through the now silent village.

Katica could feel the heavy thoughts of the other villagers. Was it safe for her to take her girls out of hiding? She pushed upward on the wood door in the floor above her. The thick rug folded back as she kept pushing the secret door open.

Matej was the first to climb the short ladder up into the house. As he reached the top he glanced around the room, his concerned eyes searched for safety. No hateful men lurked in corners of his home. Matej motioned for his family to come. His face was distorted with the anger he could not express. Matej could not allow his family to witness more violence. He suppressed and controlled his hatred, at the attacks on the people around him.

Katica encouraged Mirjana and Maria as they took hesitant steps up the ladder. Once again the girls stood on the faded rag rug that covered the secret door. Mirjana, being more bold, looked deeply into Maria's eyes. Maria's face stared at the floor.

Within minutes Katica took the girls, held them close to her, so close she could hear and feel their hearts beating. Katica's eyes turned to small pools of liquid as she watched Mirjana and Maria's faces. Young girls' faces etched with fear, concern and worry. Mirjana spoke first, "Mama, what happened? Who was here?"

Shy, sometimes subdued, Maria said with wisdom beyond her years, "We must find Papa!"

CHAPTER 4

A LETTER OF IMPORTANCE

Maria's words pounded in Katica's head all night as they attempted to sleep after their chilling ordeal. Three long years had passed since her husband was forced to leave them!

The past several years were filled with the strength and love of her parents. On the surface they lived each day snatching small moments of joy for each other and especially for Mirjana and Maria. Below their surface emotions, doubt and fear tore at them.

It was like this every night for Katica. Her thoughts would relive the day - followed by anxiety for their future. She would turn from one side to the other as the dark hours of night passed. A child's wisdom, Maria was right. Katica needed to reach Anton.

In the crystal clear light of dawn, Katica knew she must write the most important letter of her life. The graveness of the situation drove her words. Katica wrote of the increasing guerrilla raids on their Croatian village. Tito, the Yugoslavian leader of the Partisans, struck with hateful fury.

With tears in her beautiful eyes, her hand shook slightly as Katica continued to write. Her words spilled onto the paper about the village men who resisted. They were shot in the chest if they tried to stop the Partisans. Other villagers who ran to their families sometimes glanced over their shoulder. With lightning speed, bullets struck their backs.

The fateful letter was completed and sent by post. Katica thought of her letter piled with many others. It was probably on a train rumbling across tracks that took her written words to Anton. She knew the letter would take two to three long weeks to reach him. The mail was often interrupted by the frequent bombings of the railroad tracks.

He would not be surprised or shocked when he read it. Anton knew that cruel raids had happened in other villages. Anton was a good man, a man of quality who had a plan of action. His last whispered words to Katica, "Write a letter to me, if life gets too bad."

Katica did not know if her letter would reach her beloved Anton. Each day she listened to the incessant questions from her daughters. Mirjana was always the first, "Mother, do you think the letter has arrived yet? Please, please tell me!"

"Mirjana, I don't know, I just don't know."

Mirjana stomped her foot and walked away as her long,

dark hair swayed back and forth. Maria was silent for a moment before she spoke softly. "Mama, we are scared. We don't know what will happen to us."

"Maria, do you know what my last words of the letter said to your father?" Maria moved her head back and forth. "No," she said with her troubled eyes looking downward.

Katica responded, "Come home immediately!"

****

The year was 1943 as tension soared in Croatia, Europe and the entire world. Katica's letter traveled from Croatia to a barrack in Austria. Anton received the letter after three weeks. He struggled to comprehend the time. The last three years were a blur of ripped clothing being reused as he mended the German military uniforms. His daughters would now be eight and six years old. Anton would not think about Katica's age or his own.

He paced to a corner of the small room to read her letter. Anton tried to stay calm and clear. His head felt strange as if his thoughts battled each other for the correct solution. Katica's letter was important, clear and concise. He must take action and return to help his family. How could he do that?

Anton wanted to shout, "If I desert I will be shot!" He had to endure his thoughts in silence.

At last his mind cleared with an idea. He would tell the men in control of the barracks that his mother was very sick. Would they accept it? Anton would try to convince them by looking directly into their eyes. He must act confident and truthful despite the rigid tension he felt inside.

Compelled to take action, Anton approached the men in charge. As planned, he stared into the depths of their cold eyes. "I have word that my mother is frail and very sick. Could you give me the needed papers to leave the barracks to see her?"

The two burly men stared at each other as they determined their answer. Anton shifted his weight from one leg to the other as he waited. "I say only three days of clearance," the taller man shouted. The second man's thick beard moved slightly as he agreed with some reluctance.

Time blurred as Anton packed a small suitcase and boarded the train. Hours could not pass fast enough as the heavy wheels rolled along the metal rails. He fell into a state of semi-sleep interrupted by the danger around him.

The passenger train rolled along, mile after long mile. Anton woke and stared through the train's windows. Some vineyards still grew in verdant rows with luscious purple and green grapes dangling from the vines.

Virgin forests still surrounded the great Manor House where Royalty resided. Often, this royal family lived in Paris. At other times they spent months enjoying life in the huge, vine-covered stone home in Croatia.

Anton was getting close to what used to be home. His heart, his mind wanted to release intense feelings of sadness mixed with fear. Soon he would see Katica and his sweet daughters. A bitter excitement rose in his chest.

Anton's thoughts were immediately smashed as his

eyes peered through the train's windows. In the village square, a pile of German bodies was stretched out.

A shout of horror came from the man seated behind Anton. "Look, look, they cut stars in the men's scalps." The blood stained "stars" cut into human flesh made the point. The bold, red star was the grave mark, the symbol of Communism for all to witness.

It was at this very precise moment in time that Anton understood the immense importance of the letter. The violent attacks had happened for the last two years but now they were increasing.

Katica's timing for her letter was perfect. Her call for help was heard and acted upon by her husband. Anton could not wait to get to Katica and the girls.

The train ground to a full stop. Anton raced down the aisle to the door. He was the first to jump from his ride. His legs felt frozen as if he was moving in slow motion. His thoughts traveled faster than he could make his body move. His mind vibrated with the words he could not say. "I must reach her. I have to get there." He would not allow failure to happen.

Anton bumped into people as his feet raced over the cobblestone streets. "Sorry, so sorry," Anton's quick words of apology reflected his thoughts. His pace quickened – his heart pounded in his chest.

At last Anton realized he was about a block from Katica's parents' home. He lunged forward until he felt his lungs would burst. There it was, their home was just ahead.

His pace slowed as Anton's eyes darted around the

street, yard and house. Clues of suspicious action could be anywhere. He had an elevated, alert mind focused on the immense, crucial objective – get his family out.

There was no knock on the door, Anton walked boldly in. He found them all huddled together in one room. Their anxiety and tension filled the air.

When Anton's eyes met Katica's, they both fought emotions that tried to pour out. Anton choked his rush of love with firm words, "We have to leave. Pack one bag."

With a small ray of love in his voice, "Girls, help your mother. We need to go right now!"

A mixture of joy and confusion covered Mirjana's and Maria's faces. Katica wanted to pack with some organization, but there was no time, no choice.

Katica heard the urgency in Anton's voice. "Come Katica, girls, the train is waiting!"

****

Once again a cloak of heavy sadness covered Katica, Mirjana and Maria as they hugged Hannah and Matej. An intense good-bye from Katica to her parents ended. The farewell between the girls and their beloved grandparents was so difficult to watch that Katica turned away.

Would they ever see each other again? Only time held the answer.

CHAPTER 5

TO EXIST IN AUSTRIA

They walked, hands held together, past the homes of their neighbors. At times, Anton could not resist putting his younger daughter, Maria, on his strong shoulders. She giggled a little when he picked her up. Maria was with her father at last. She did not know, it was only for a moment in time.

Soon they could smell the heavy smoke from the train. As the family rounded the corner, they could see the long rows of passenger cars hooked together. It seemed to wait with impatience for the load of passengers.

Katica clasped the girls' hands more firmly to help prepare them for what would happen soon. Anton bent over, held both of their small faces and kissed them with great affection. He turned to Katica, with one swift embrace Anton held her in his arms. The love between them was deeper than words could express. He released her slowly and stepped onto the train.

A gruff man approached Katica, "Woman, you need to board the next section of the train. Hurry those girls along."

Mirjana and Maria's frightened eyes pleaded with their mother. Mirjana was the first to speak, "Mother, where do we go, what should we do?"

Maria whimpered, "Why did Papa leave us? Where is he now?"

Another door of the train rattled open. "Hurry, girls, it is time." Katica coaxed them into the train – she longed to push away their fear.

Katica sat in the small shabby train seat with her two daughters packed together beside her. She bent close to them. "I know a lot has happened so quickly. We'll talk together when we get there."

With some impatience, Mirjana had to ask, "But Mama where are we going?" Katica distracted them, "Look out the train windows. There is plenty to see."

Maria, with a little courage, said, "The train windows are dirty. How can we see?"

Katica could feel the corners of her mouth turn up slightly. She felt a small amount of hope in the words of her younger daughter. "Yes, the windows were smudged with dirt, but I want you to see new things, people and places you've never experienced," Katica tried to place adventure into her voice.

They watched the stucco houses, influenced by Germanic architecture, as the train rushed past them. And then Katica saw it....

With a quick, short breath and then a sigh, she smothered her emotions. The unknown thoughts hidden behind Katica's beautiful dark eyes would remain there. No one would ever know. Her deep, steady gaze saw the large impressive Manor House. The grand home was long with many windows to view the land of Croatia. Dark, green ivy vines caressed the entire exterior.

With excitement in her voice, Mirjana spoke. "Look Mama, the two very tall towers on both ends of the Manor House."

"I know, I see them. They are watch towers to see people in the distance coming to our part of Croatia," Katica answered.

****

Katica remembered how she and her mother, Hannah, had saved the cream off the top of the milk to make rich, thick butter. More than one time, Hannah had Katica take their delicious butter to the Manor House to sell.

Katica always knew what to do. She remembered to use the servant's door, never the main entrance door. Her thoughts continued back in time.

On several occasions, Katica recalled approaching the weather-worn heavy wood door. It creaked as it opened. She stood there with timid humility. Katica wore a simple peasant blouse. The sunlight fell on her wavy, long hair creating highlights of color. In her hands Katica held the pottery crock of warm, sweet butter.

The servant who opened the door smiled slightly and said, "Hello, we've been waiting for your butter. I can't always be here to answer your knock on the door."

"I know, it's my job to find you," Katica replied.

As they talked, Katica caught a glimpse of him, the Noble's son. He was an impressive man, tall and handsome. As he walked from one elegant room to the next, the son of nobility carried himself well. His masculine swagger could not be denied.

Katica's interested eyes lowered their gaze to the polished stone floor. He must not see her looking at him. Now if only she could stop the pink blush in her cheeks.

The servant woman retrieved a couple of coins from her pocket and placed them in Katica's hand. The thought of this simple gesture from a time long ago, brought Katica back to the reality of today.

****

The train continued its journey on the thick metal track. Katica pushed a strand of hair away from her eye and looked at her girls. She sensed Mirjana and Maria needed reassurance. A chaotic mixture of sadness, separation, and fear bubbled in their minds.

"Mirjana, Maria, I know so much has happened but I want you to remember one important thing. I promise I'll always be with you."

"Mama, how can you be sure?" asked Mirjana.

"With all my heart and all my power, you both are more important than anything else in this world." It was the only response Katica could give.

A sudden thought struck her — the beauty and intrigue

of the stately Manor House was only about five miles from their home. That lifetime was completely vanished.

As their long train lumbered along its path, the small family of three did not realize what was happening in their village. The year was 1944 and by October the eight hundred villagers were evacuated.

Katica's parents, Hannah and Matej, had climbed into a large, old wooden wagon. Two dappled gray hoses pulled them away from the town and life they used to love.

They focused on the docile horses that pulled their wagon to safety. By night flickering yellow light from the wagon's lanterns cut through the depths of darkness.

The strong yet gentle horses seemed to know their duty – to know the way. On some long nights the welcome moonlight bathed them in light. Matej and Hannah searched for hope in the delicate shadows of tree branches etched on the land. Their hope was to reach the country of Austria.

It could have been two separate dreams, experienced by two different women, Katica and her mother, Hannah. In the harsh reality of the mid 1940's, it was the clear, vivid truth.

Young, beautiful Katica with her two daughters rode in a passenger train to Austria. Katica's parents, Hannah and Matej, also traveled to Austria. Their journey was in a covered wagon that rolled along on wooden wheels.

Would the families ever meet again or would they be lost in another place, another time? Circumstances for both had forced them to leave behind the most important documents of their lives. Birth records, Baptismal Dates and Marriage Certificates had been abandoned to history!

CHAPTER 6

A LIFE IN HIDING

In the rush of meeting and a short precious time together, another sad departure had happened. Anton in this short space of time had shoved a small, paper note into Katica's pocket.

As she attempted to recover from the loss of her love again, her hand slipped into this same pocket. Katica's slender fingers touched the paper. She brought it out just enough to read his words. Katica closed her eyes for a few moments after she absorbed the contents. There was an address written followed by the words – attic room!

Anton had managed to find a room for them. How had he accomplished this in the space of three short days?

A slight smile tugged at the corners of Katica's mouth. "Mirjana, Maria, your father found a room for us to live in."

It no longer mattered that the train's windows were dirty or of more importance that fear and violence surrounded them. Anton had given them hope, in the humble form of a small white paper.

As the long train rumbled along the rails, Katica's thoughts could not stay away from the Manor House the train had passed. There were so many windows in the large stone home. She remembered the black, wrought iron fence that stood in protection of the home where nobility lived. The Baron of the House had said, "Our main home in Paris is our chateau."

She must stop thinking of the Manor House and her old home in a more humble section of the village. Katica focused on the present time where a train was taking them to Austria.

Minutes, followed by hours, crept by. After a while Mirjana spoke, "Mama, when can we get off this train?"

Maria joined in, "I'm tired of sitting in this seat."

Katica understood, her response was filled with empathy. "I know, girls. We should be in Austria soon. Be still a little longer." In her heart Katica knew, although they blamed the train, their real feelings churned inside. They had experienced too much terror for their young ages.

As the countryside rushed past them, their heads nodded, their eyes closed and sleep calmed them. Katica rested also.

Sometime later their train jolted to a stop. Katica's eyes opened with the sudden stop in motion. Her gentle words woke her daughters, "Mirjana, Maria, I think we are here." She coaxed them from their sleep.

A man, dressed all in gray, spoke with a mixture of authority and melancholy, "You all must get off here. This way down the aisle."

"Come girls, we are here in Austria."

Apprehension filled Katica as they stepped off the train. She had never been in another country before. Her familiar Croatia became yet another memory. A new life in Austria began. What would it be like?

The evening light was fading. She needed to find the address Anton had given her. Confused people surrounded Katica. Her eyes scanned the ones beyond the train passengers.

Katica noticed a pleasant-looking woman about her own age. She looked like someone Katica could approach. "Hello, could you tell me where to find this area of town?" Katica showed the small note that was so important.

The stranger responded without hesitation, "Walk to the end of this neighborhood. Keep walking until you come to the house near the forest." She smiled and connected with Katica's eyes. "They are a good family." A slight rapport flowed between the two women.

"Well, girls, after sitting for so long, we are going for a walk," Katica said. The dirt road was soft under their feet and the forest beyond beckoned them.

Katica clutched the small bag stuffed with their clothing. She considered what life would be like in Austria. This country seemed a long distance from Croatia where Tito and the Partisans and Hitler with his men forced their ambitions and ideas upon all.

They walked toward the home near the thick woods. The last rays of a burning, orange sunset flickered through the trees. Katica quickened her pace so she could reach the house first. Her daughters were only a short distance behind.

A hopeful Katica knocked on the front door of a well-kept home. As the door opened, a woman with concern in her voice spoke, "I see you are the lady with the young daughters. I expected you to arrive around this time."

"Yes, you have an attic room for us," Katica replied.

"You need to come back in a few days. It is important that you wait," the woman said.

Her words lingered in the fresh air of the country where pine trees grew a short distance away. Katica's hope evaporated as she spoke, "Please keep the room for us. We will come back."

Katica reached for the girls' hands as they turned and walked back. "Somehow we have to be brave." She paused and looked at their young, beautiful faces. "Mirjana, Maria, we will do this together and stay safe." At their young ages of nine and seven, they had experienced too much fear and terror.

They trudged along the road back to the village. Although the train had continued its journey, some local people still remained. One curious peasant woman looked at Katica. "Could I help you?" she said. "Yes," Katica answered. "Is there a hotel here in the village?"

"There is, near the center of town," the woman replied. She pointed the way; she knew she had helped in a small way.

Katica nodded a thank you with a smile. She had managed to save a small amount of money that Anton had sent home to her. His work of ripping apart old shirts to mend German military uniforms was being used.

The welcome lights of the hotel were only a short

distance away. "Well, girls, I hope there is a room for us here." They had no words as they looked at their mother's tired face. Katica was still a beautiful woman despite their grueling ordeal.

Minutes passed as they walked into the modest but clean hotel. Katica spoke to a lady sitting behind a fine, old desk. "Could we rent a room for about four days?"

Katica was quick to show money in the open palm of her hand. The hotel woman reached for a pull handle on a wooden drawer. It held an old yet shiny key. "Here is the key to your room," she said. "The number is on the back."

Katica held the antique key and wondered what would happen behind the door it opened. Their bodies ached, their eyelids were heavy as they climbed the long, wooden staircase.

Soon Katica turned the key in the lock that opened the thick door to their room. They felt a small sense of security and privacy in their clean room.

"Oh, I'm so tired," Katica sighed, "we should all get some rest." The beds looked so appealing with soft blankets and several pillows piled high.

"Mother, you sleep in the large bed. Maria and I can share the other one," Mirjana said.

Feelings of exhaustion overtook them as they snuggled under the thick blankets. A sliver of light from a single moonbeam passed through a space in the window coverings.

"I was just wondering how long we are going to wait before we go back to the house," Mirjana said.

Katica wiped a small tear from the corner of her eye.

"I don't know. I'll talk to the hotel people and bring some food back to you."

As she walked downstairs, Katica felt a small amount of guilt. She was always honest with her daughters. This time she was not. The money that Anton had sent her was almost gone. She chose not to compound their fears with more uncertainty.

Two pleasant women behind the old wood desk watched Katica as she approached them. "Did you sleep well?" one of the ladies asked.

"We slept very well. Could I ask for something to eat, just a little something?" Katica asked.

"Of course, come with me to the kitchen." She gave toast and a small bowl of bright, red strawberries to Katica.

"Thank you, may I ask you a question?" Katica felt like a beggar.

Without letting Katica continue, she spoke, "We could use your help washing dishes for a few days."

Katica was quick to reply, "I am so grateful." Her words were sincere yet Katica's emotions forced her eyes to stare at the floor.

"Come back to the kitchen after you eat with your daughters."

"I will, thank you again," Katica said.

She hurried back to the room and slid the old key into the tarnished lock. As she opened the door Katica again saw a now natural concern on their faces. "Look, come and eat, I brought toast and fresh strawberries for us."

The toast was no longer warm yet it still tasted so good.

"Mother, the strawberries are so juicy and delicious," Maria said. Mirjana smiled, with a little juice on her chin.

"Girls, I'm going to work in the kitchen for a few days while we are here. I would like you both to try to relax, rest and talk to each other about everything. Maybe it will help," said Katica. She walked away from them towards the door. "Oh, one more thought, just to be safe, I'm going to lock you in." Katica wished the last words had not escaped from her mouth.

Mirjana and Maria looked at each other and back to their mother. The small clue from Katica hinted at the real situation they were living. With the click of the door lock they settled into the routine of the next several days. They were together at times. Often Katica worked in the hotel kitchen while the girls spent quiet time together in the room. It was hours of reflection about all that had happened and what was yet to come.

On the fourth evening, Katica came back to their room with bread and vegetables. As they ate the small meal Katica spoke, "I have overheard guests speaking that it seems to be a safe time in the village. I think we should try to get the attic room again."

Mirjana always managed to talk first, "Yes, Mama, yes. Let's go tomorrow."

"Do you agree Maria?" Katica asked.

"Yes, it is time to go. We feel like we are hiding here and that no one should see us." Maria stared at the floor as she talked. At times her shyness showed even with her mother and sister.

Katica sensed there was more that Maria wanted to say. "What else Maria?"

Maria began, "Today we found the doll in the bottom of your bag. We remembered a long time ago when we played with her." The doll's beautiful, porcelain face and soft body called to both of them. "We both pulled too hard, Mama." Maria started to cry and talk at the same time. "We both wanted to hold the doll. We're sorry Mama, our doll broke." Sometimes it takes one last small thing to make the tears flow.

Katica understood as she spoke with the gentle tone of a mother. "When I packed a few clothes for us, I noticed the doll and I just grabbed her. Couldn't help it. I thought she might hold happy memories for you."

She continued, "Let's get some sleep so we can leave right away in the morning. We'll put your doll in the bottom of the bag just as she is."

As night deepened they slept for hours. Morning rays of sunshine woke them. "Girls, let's go to the kitchen and say our thank you's and good-byes." They stuffed their few belongings into the bag.

In the kitchen there were a few words and quick hugs. Katica's steps were deliberate and strong as she walked from the hotel with her daughters.

The fresh air filled their lungs and the sunlight caressed their skin. It felt so good to walk the land. Katica, Mirjana and Maria strolled along as they savored every moment. It was less than an hour's walk to the house near the woods.

"Mother, there is the house," Mirjana said. Katica's eyes swept over the many beautiful trees close to them.

The greenery, the branches, the wind whispered through the leaves and pine needles. It all reminded Katica of the virgin forests of her Croatia that she was forced to leave.

Soon they were on the porch and ready to knock. The door swung open and the same pleasant lady welcomed them inside. "Come, you can have your room now," she said.

A feeling of relief settled on them as they followed the home-owner up the stairway. She turned to Katica. "You understand that your room is in the attic." Katica nodded, "Yes, I do, it's fine."

After one more flight of steep stairs they arrived in the attic. Between the wood beams and wooden walls stood a medium sized door. The lady spoke again, "We will do our best to keep you safe." With these few words she left them.

A small table with a single light gave a soft glow to the large dark attic. "Well girls, let's open the latch and go in. This could be our home for awhile. Maria's eyes widened. "Mama, I think I heard someone in there, behind the door."

"There shouldn't be. Your father secured this room for us. Listen for a minute," Katica said.

They stared at the attic door. Apprehension filled every breath they took. Someone was behind the old, attic door. Katica extended her arm and pressed her thumb down on the latch. The girls stood close to Katica and stared straight ahead. The door creaked open with unbearable slowness.

Katica, Mirjana and Maria were shocked with disbelief. Their fears were sliced apart; joy rushed in. Katica's parents, Matej and Hannah, stood before them. Katica almost shouted, "How did you get here? When did you come?"

CHAPTER 7

THE ATTIC INTERLUDE

No words were needed from Matej and Hannah. Their faces, especially their eyes, glowed with tranquility. The old dark attic with exposed wood rafters in the pitched ceiling transformed into a place of joy.

"Mother, Father, you are here! I can't believe all of this," exclaimed Katica, Mirjana and Maria as they rushed to hug them. They were so thrilled to see their grandparents – it was difficult to end their embraces.

"Mother, what happened? How did you get here first?" Katica asked.

"Come, let's all sit on the bed. I'll tell you the story," Hannah began. She looked into Katica's eyes and drew closer to her granddaughters, Maria and Mirjana. "We heard talk around our village," Hannah continued. "The high anti-German resentment was building because of the German occupation of Croatia. We feared more violence." Hannah looked downward, "There were nine hundred people in the village." Their eyes locked together as their minds made the large decision.

Matej interjected, "There was no choice. We had to leave and as soon as possible."

Hannah and Matej recalled the hard work of loading the wagon. Armful after armful of food, clothing and bedding were packed and put in place. Both were grateful that they owned two strong horses and a wagon. Everyone in the village did not have this way of leaving, only those who farmed.

The story continued as Hannah began speaking again. "We were one of the first to go."

"Let me tell this part," Matej broke in. Katica and the girls' attention focused back and forth between them. "We stood outside the home where we had lived so many years together. Our eyes shifted to our horses that would carry us and a few belongings to another place and another time. It was then that the German military marched around the corner and down our street. We froze in place like statues. With rigid leg and arm movements the men came closer. The military were soon upon us."

One uniformed officer stood forward. "Where are you going?" he barked.

In quick reply, Matej spoke back. "We have children in Austria. We're going to join them." The gruff military man motioned them forward.

Hannah and Matej had stepped up and into the large wagon. Matej grasped the reins – the horses knew what to do. Hannah glanced over her shoulder at their family home. Matej could not look. His feelings of loss and regret became a shroud over his eyes.

Katica, Mirjana and Maria heard the words of their loved ones yet it became a vivid scene that took action before them. They listened more as the past few days happened again in their minds.

Matej's next words were heavy. "The German military escorted us out of Croatia. Tears stung our eyes as we fought not to cry in front of them."

In almost a whisper, Maria asked, "Opa, Oma, what happened next?"

Hannah answered, "Your grandfather's steady hands guided our horses and I sat on all the contents in the over-loaded wagon. I tried to separate myself from the food. The five gallon brass cans of meat surrounded me."

"Oh, Mother, this brings a memory of Croatia to me," Katica said. "Remember every autumn the pigs were butchered and the lard was boiled?"

"Oh, yes and the air smelled of boiled meat and maybe the blood too," replied Hannah.

Mirjana answered, "I remember we poured the hot lard over the meat to preserve it."

Maria just had to get into the conversation. "The people put blocks of ice in the hay to keep the food good too."

Faint smiles spread across their faces. They all remembered the baking. Every two weeks they baked bread in the brick ovens outdoors. The special little loaves were for the children and cake and cookies for everyone.

Hannah spoke once again, "Always remember girls,

your great-grandfather made many of those brick ovens. He was considered very good at it."

"We'll remember, Oma," both girls said together.

Katica's turn to talk came, "Back to what happened and how you got here."

Hannah's words tumbled out, "Anton found a way to put a note in your father's pocket too. I wrote to the people who had an attic room."

"By daylight we traveled through Croatia's green belt where vegetables and beautiful vineyards grew, heavy with red, purple and green grapes. On cloud filled days, large raindrops pelted the canopy over our wagon. With the darkness of night we continued by the swaying light of our wagon lanterns." Hannah's thought–filled words mesmerized them all.

Matej had to end the spell of her words as he said, "We witnessed the cruel work of the Partisans again. The body of a German military officer hung from a telephone wire beside the road. His blood had not completely dried. This stressed our need to leave Croatia and our home." Again, another hateful display of terrorism.

"Enough," Katica's voice cut through the air. "We must think of this time, this moment. We found each other – we're together!"

In a gradual sequence they all fell into sleep. It was a bittersweet reunion in a large attic room.

Outside, after dawn, light crept along the land. There were no windows in the attic to know it was a new day. Katica's nose twitched a little as she wondered what she was smelling. It was an old house smell, almost musty. Oh, yes, we're in an attic – she remembered.

The stale air of the third floor of the house gave the women an immediate chore. They scrubbed the floors with an intensity that released many emotions chained inside them. They attempted to change the smell of every breath they took. As the hours of the first day passed, the family soon realized the new truth. Their time in the attic would be a secret life.

The stillness, the lack of something to fill their days, replaced raw fear. Waves of new emotions washed over them. The joy of being together was dampened by the lack of freedom.

Sometimes Mirjana and Maria attempted to communicate with facial expressions. That only lasted so long. Mirjana spoke out, "I wish there were books to read in this attic."

Maria answered, "So do I. Life seems so simple up here. We can't make any noise or talk much."

"Mother doesn't want to take a chance that we are asked to leave," Mirjana said.

Grandmother Hannah walked closer to the girls. "Now girls, what is the grumbling? There are some days your father manages to come for a little while. He stops sewing the military uniforms and brings us some food from the base," Hannah said.

The girls tried to act appreciative. When Anton had left them with such abruptness, his main objective was to get back to the German base within his time allowance. He had been on emergency leave and had no permission to bring his family to Austria. Anton could not live with them. Their secret life continued.

Silence lingered in the air only for a short time. "I need to find work on one of the area farms," Katica said. "Would you two like to walk into the village with me?" she asked.

"Oh, yes, Mama, maybe we could find some fresh food," Mirjana just had to say.

"Let's go right now. The fresh air and sunlight will do us so much good," Katica said.

Hannah and Matej watched as the three left their attic hide-away. With Katica leading, Mirjana and Maria walked with cautious steps down the two flights of steep stairs. The fresh air and sunlight intoxicated them as they came into the village after their long walk.

Only two market vendors waited for buyers on this particular sun-lit morning. Katica's eyes brightened as she said, "Look, juicy plums and fresh green beans."

The girls were so pleased when they heard their mother speak, "Could I have one small box of each?"

This one sale made the peasant lady smile in gratitude as Katica paid for the fresh food. "Thank you," she said, "the plums and green beans were picked this morning."

With their treasures of food clutched in their hands, they began their hike back to the attic room. The call and sounds of birds added to the pleasure of being outdoors as they walked along.

An ominous feeling overtook Katica as the wind grew strong and bold. She tried to shake away the silent fear as the wind intensified. Soon the house was in their view. "Hurry, girls, we're almost there."

In Katica's mind, the chilling wind gusts seemed to be an omen of danger. She must concentrate on their attic life.

They hurried into the house and once again climbed the long wooden stairs.

"Oma, Opa, we brought fresh food for dinner," Mirjana said with excitement.

With gratitude they enjoyed the soup made from the green beans, the plums, and their usual food from the wagon. After dinner and the long walk into the village, Katica and her girls fell into a deep sleep.

As the next day dawned, a pattern of attic days continued. Sometimes they sang familiar songs. Other times Grandmother told stories. Grandfather always had to okay the stories. He was still the dominate head of the family. When irritation levels rose between Mirjana and Maria, Grandfather raised his voice. The young ladies shriveled when he reprimanded them.

Day after day their attic existence dragged on. They all came to acceptance as the months inched forward to a full year. This simple, secret life would soon be shattered.

CHAPTER 8

FROM QUIET ATTIC TO THE SOUND OF WAR

The sudden gusts of strong wind had stirred a premonition in Katica. In a short space of time the foreboding feeling unfolded. There was a cautious knock on the attic door.

Mirjana jumped in response to open the old door. The lady who owned the house stood there. Her face was somber, her words filled with concern. "The war surrounds us. The bombs are getting closer. I wanted you to know."

Mirjana and Maria looked at each other with fear. With down-cast eyes the lady left as she closed the door behind her.

Before the impact of her words had settled in their minds, there was a second knock. She began again, "I'm sorry, the Russians know you are here. Be careful."

There was an unspoken bond between the home owners and Katica's family. They shared the strong will to survive.

Matej spoke, "There will be sirens to warn us if bombs are dropping." He paused, "The man of the house told me. He said we should run to the woods."

Four strong women, young and old, reached for each other's hands. "We must be ready, all the time," Mirjana said.

The second night after the heavy news, the front door was forced open! With loud ominous footsteps the men thundered up the stairs. One Russian soldier shouted, "Where are they?"

Another Russian answered, "I heard there are young women here. We can take what we want." An evil look overtook his face.

"No, not this time," the leader said, "the man here speaks Slavic. We might need him."

They burst into the attic room and stared at Katica's family as they stood still, frozen in fear. Neither group of people seemed to know what to do. Cold looks passed between anyone who looked at another.

With a shock of braveness, Matej spoke. "I have coffee. I can put a shot of whiskey in it."

Hannah and Katica could not believe what Matej had just said. Violence and rape waited in the hands of the intruders to grab and force their wicked ways on the women. What could Matej have been thinking?

The tense, bizarre nightmare played out in the attic. Katica and Hannah moved the young girls to the far edges of the large, upper room. Matej sipped coffee with his hidden motive to protect his family. The Russian men gulped the whiskey spiked coffee as they asked Matej war-related questions.

They charged away with the abruptness of their entrance. One shouted out, "We'll be back." The night's ordeal ended.

The following morning did not give them the chance to discuss the strange event of last night - instead the sharp sound of sirens blast through the air. Without words Matej gathered his family.

They raced down the wooden staircase with anxiety building with each step. Maria spoke, "I want to go faster but I don't want to fall."

Hannah replied, "I'm so slow. Katica, take the girls, go ahead to the woods."

Mirjana's lips trembled, "The sirens are relentless, bombs must be coming."

Matej pushed them forward towards the forest. His Hannah had caught up. They heard the hiss of a bomb as it sliced through the sky. Only a short distance away it thundered to the ground. Fear pierced their hearts as they ran faster and faster.

The bright, deep green of the woods was just before them – never had it looked so beautiful. The home owners were there before them. Their arms waved in rapid motion as they showed the location of the bunker. "Hurry, hurry," they shouted.

Mirjana was the first to arrive at the edge of the hidden bunker. It had been dug deep into the forest floor with a tough rope to help them get in.

Maria, her face white with fear, was lowered into the hole first. Hannah rubbed against the dirt walls as she dropped into hiding.

In the shady corner, on the dark, damp floor stood a large black pot. Mirjana noticed it and managed to avoid bumping into the steaming pot as she climbed into the earth.

All seven were now in the partial safety of the underground bunker. Sarah and Peter, the house family, and Matej's family huddled together. Matej was the last one in – he reached his long arms outward and pulled pine boughs over the opening. His arms were scratched from the needles of pine branches and the prickly rope fibers.

They sat on the soil and waited. Sarah broke the silence, "Would anyone like a cup of potato soup? I even had one sausage to cook into the soup." Peter encouraged them to eat. "Sarah made it early this morning to be ready in case the bombs came." She ladled out a steaming cup for each of them. Despite the harsh conditions the warm soup tasted delicious as it rolled over their tongues. Hannah thought to herself....I believe Sarah has done this before.

Early that morning Hannah had helped Sarah transfer the potato soup from the farmhouse kitchen stove to a slim, metal milk can. Before the war the women traveled to the nearest dairy for the family's milk. The milk cans had been containers of nourishment. Now, during the war, they became vessels of food for survival.

The air raid sirens screeched on! Their fear deepened as their minds reacted to the sound of the bombs and the damp, musty smell of the earth around them. Mirjana shouted out, "We just ran for our lives!"

Maria, in a more quiet tone asked, "What will happen to us?" The women stared at each other with anxious eyes.

The comfort of the potato soup was shattered. A bomb exploded, near to them, maybe just a few miles away. Maria's eyes pleaded as she said, "I'm so scared, are we going to die?" Katica held her close.

Hour after hour crept by as the pace of the bombs slowed. The earth moved beneath them as they heard and felt the impacts. The beauty of the forest, the safety of the bunker, changed to a small underground prison.

When night overtook the land, the air raid sirens ended the warning. With caution each one climbed out of their forest sanctuary. The stars still sparkled in the dark night sky that had been disturbed by the destructive bombs of war. Matej's thoughts deepened as he walked back to the house with his family and friends. The great green virgin forests, an endless black sky studded with diamonds of light, there was so much beauty around them. The actions of people, who could not live with the beliefs of people different from their own, disgusted him. Violence, destruction, death – how many centuries will pass before life changes? Children's blood-soaked bodies do not even stop it.

Ice water must flow through their hearts, not the warm blood filled with emotions of care. Matej's anger of the day erupted inside him!

CHAPTER 9

A JOURNEY TO THE FUTURE

The bombs made the decision – it was time to leave the attic! As they rushed back into the house, their eyes searched each other's faces for clues of what to do next. Matej spoke first, "As frightened as you are, I want you to sleep. I will give all of this deep thought and have a decision for you in the morning."

Mirjana answered, "But how can we sleep?" Their troubled grandfather sat in a small chair. The rays of the setting sun slipped below the horizon. Matej responded with a low voice, "You must all sleep."

Only a few minutes later an urgent knock sounded on the door. Shy Maria with an unusual show of boldness opened the door. The heavy atmosphere of despair in the stale, attic air changed in this moment in time. Their beloved Anton stood before them!

The words shot out of his mouth, "The base has been bombed! Do you still have the horses and wagon?"

"Yes," they all said at once. Each one of them filled with emotions of love, relief and confusion. Katica, the strong, beautiful wife and mother poured out her words, "I cannot express all that I am feeling. My mind could explode with it all." She rushed to Anton, put her arms around him and held him close. Tears poured from her lovely eyes and over her cheeks. "I can't ever lose you. We must keep the family together!"

Anton answered, "With all my strength, we will be together."

Katica and Anton released each other with great tenderness. Anton faced them all. "I'm coming with you. My job is gone. There is no need for a tailor," Anton said. A faint feeling of hope passed among them. In the morning light, they would load the wagon. They had experienced the last bombs. The strength of the Allies had triumphed, good over evil.

The war had ended! Austria was divided into the Russian Zone, the British Zone, and the American Zone. This time their wagon wheels rolled over land scarred by war.

Matej and Anton sat in the front as they guided the horses. They held the horses' reins with the tightness of their mindset. Determination to keep their family safe and together was etched in their faces.

"Are we going back to Croatia?" Katica asked.

"Yes, but I'm not sure what we will find," Anton answered.

Their wagon rolled past blackened earth, crumbled

buildings and destroyed homes. It seemed like they could almost reach into the air and pull out sadness.

A short distance away, a small group of people stood together. Mirjana said, "I'm not sure what's happening with those people."

Katica noticed they waved their arms and pointed fingers. Out from the center, a Russian military stood. With crisp, cold words, he shouted, "This land is under Russian command. Get ready to return to your own countries."

Anxiety and confusion settled into the people. All the refugees near Matej and Anton's family strained to hear the Russian leader's words, "Croatians, form into a transport. You'll travel by horse and wagon to southern Austria."

The heavy impact of World War II touched their souls and refused to leave. As the long, difficult road to the border of Yugoslavia began, Katica's mind drifted back to her life in the small Croatian village. There was so much for her mind to process yet a persistent, pleasant thought returned again and again. She still pictured the handsome nobleman in the Manor House. He was a tall, impressive man who walked with the air of nobility. Despite his place in life, there was a hint of mischief in his attractive pale, blue eyes. A small smile tugged at the corners of her mouth. With silent words she said, "Stop, stop it, you must not think of him!"

The wagons rolled on and on with the strong horses bearing more responsibility than even their people understood. Maria touched her mother's arm. "We've been in the wagon for a long time. There's a section of land with trees," Maria said. "Could I run over there and catch up with the wagon train?"

Hannah responded with understanding before Katica could answer. "Of course you can dear. I'll be watching for you." Grandmother Hannah's eyes stayed on Maria until she entered the small woods.

Katica and Hannah knew their time would come to go into the wooded area. Their gaze locked on the thick, dense trees. The minutes seemed to stop as they waited to see Maria. At last she came from behind the trees with a disgusted look on her young, beautiful face. Her long, slender legs ran across the field to the wagon.

Hour after hour the wagons rumbled across the once beautiful land toward the Yugoslavian border. The sound of thundering hooves came towards them. The Russian man on horseback shouted, "When you reach the border, wait for the Yugoslav militia to come and get you." Anton and Matej's only answer was to nod their heads.

As they drew near the border, they soon realized they were now under British command. Anticipation of their future filled every person in every wagon. Soon the air crackled with rumor or the truth. Matej spoke, "I have to tell you, German speaking people did not return to their homes at the border. Instead, they were put in hard labor camps and families were separated!"

Matej, Hannah, Anton and Katica began the deep decision process. Mirjana and Maria looked concerned as the family discussed their options.

Anton turned his head from one side of the wagon to the other and just stared. "Matej, look around us," he said.

Matej's eyes widened. With amazement he spoke, "Katica, girls, look. There are hundreds of us." A confused, chaos of people covered the green patches of grass that still survived despite the trampling of war and now the roll of wagon wheels.

The entire family felt caught in the drama of the current situation. Hannah, with torn words, said, "I can't stand to be separated again."

Mirjana looked at Anton with great fondness. "Father, you can't go to a labor camp. I wouldn't be able to get the cruelty of your hardship out of my mind."

Maria, being the youngest of them all, ached with the meaning of their words. She looked at her father and grandfather for an answer. Anton said, "Matej, we must go to the British commander and tell him how afraid we are."

"Let's go right now. We have to take action," Matej answered.

Katica said, "Yes, go now. Mirjana and I can handle the horses."

Mirjana climbed to the front of the wagon and took the reins from her father's hands. Katica grabbed Matej's reins for the second strong horse. Both men felt the urgency in the women's actions.

As their feet touched the solid earth after the long wagon ride, the firmness of the land enforced their determination. "Matej, hurry, we must find the leader of the British command," Anton said.

"I'm coming. My old legs are stiff from sitting so long in the wagon," Matej responded. "Look ahead. The man with the longer dark hair and uniform is probably the British commander."

They approached him with caution and the confidence of two men who wanted safety for their family. Anton, with a firm tone, spoke, "We have heard about the labor camps and the family separations. We will not live with or accept this cruelty."

Matej added, "Where is your dignity? Why don't people learn the hard lessons of war?"

The British Commander stood taller and tilted his head back. He said, "You must not want to go across the border to Yugoslavia!"

"Much is still wrong there," Anton pelted back.

The British Commander added," I hear a German accent in your words."

Matej said, "We lived in a peaceful Croatian village. Some German was spoken there."

After a short pause, the British leader felt empathy. He responded, "I will not force you to go back but I must send you to a camp while we organize and decide what to do."

Anton said, "Thank you for understanding what we are experiencing. We have lost our home, our belongings, all of our important papers. We have nothing!"

Anton and Matej walked back to the safety of their wagon. As they came close to the four women who they loved from a place deep within, Anton could not hold back his words. "We are going to a British camp here in Austria. We're not going back to Croatia. There is too much danger there." Matej added, "Yes, I know it is a camp but not a hard labor camp. The most important part is we are together!" Mirjana and Maria hugged as Katica smiled.

Anton shaded his tired eyes with his hand. He looked around at the crowded field of people. "Matej, it is time to move our horses and wagon away from the others," Anton said.

"Katica and Mirjana, would you light the lanterns on the sides of our wagon?" Anton asked. "Night time is coming."

The British camp was close to the fields where they had been waiting. Their trusted horses pulled away from the hundreds of others. The bright lanterns flickered with soft light. The soft sway of the same lanterns reflected a new motion in their lives. Fear would be replaced by confinement!

As wagon wheels rolled, the lanterns lit the way through the darkness. The war had ended and confinement would begin.....

CHAPTER 10

THE AUSTERE LIFE WITHIN A CONFINEMENT CAMP

A great exodus began as wagon after wagon split away from all the others. Anton took command of their horses to steer them away from the other wagons. The animals sensed the tension around them. A loud snort warned Anton that his horses were too close to larger, more dominant horses. With quick control of the reins, he coaxed his team away.

Some wagons headed to the border of Austria and Croatia. They held on to the hope of their home in Croatia.

Others left for the land they remembered as Yugoslavia. Still others just remained still and quiet as they thought of fiery sunsets reflected on the Adriatic Sea.

Anton and Matej pulled ahead of several wagons. A

husky man in uniform ran in front of them. "Who are you? Where are you from?" he shouted.

Anton answered with a firm tone. "We have British permission to go to their camp near here."

"Go, be gone from here," the military man said.

The fields under the wagon wheels were sometimes green, some were golden like straw. Other fields were charred from war. The men, often lost in their own silence, drove the wagon onward. Mirjana and Maria were filled with anticipation. "Mirjana, what do you think the camp will be like?" Maria asked.

Mirjana answered, "I suppose we'll find out soon. At least we are together." Maria nodded with a slight smile. Katica and Hannah looked at each other with understanding and strength. The hours in the wagon passed with a slow pace.

At last Katica saw the British camp. She put her hand to her mouth as she spoke, "The camp is surrounded by a tall wire fence!"

The family stared in silence at the austere place where they would live for an indefinite amount of time. Their thoughts concentrated on the stark image of the strong, wire fence. What would their life be like behind those long walls of the camp building? The fence loomed before them as a barrier to their freedom!

Mirjana's words poured out, "Father, what does this all mean?"

Anton answered with a solemn tone, "My dear daughter, I want to say this is just a brief sojourn, but with complete honesty I'm not sure."

The long procession of horse-drawn wagons approached

the tall wire fence. With a slow swing of movement, an iron gate opened. Fear of their unknown future settled around them as they rode through the entrance.

Anton, always the strong leader of the family, focused his eyes with precision on every detail of their new surroundings. Katica spoke first, "We are all going inside together to find our place among all the others."

This did not happen. The mass of people was too large and the confusion too great. A man with a crisp British accent approached them. "You all must drive your wagons and park them in the large field near the camp."

Once again the family huddled together in their wagon. The gray sky surrendered to the darkness of night. Mirjana, in a sincere effort to be positive, said, "Maria, look at the bright stars that sparkle over us. There are so many."

They all gazed at the tiny stars like diamonds thrown across a night sky. For a few moments, Katica thought of a larger presence in the vast universe. She felt hope.

As the hours of night passed, the clouds thickened. In the morning gentle rains fell on the horses and wagons. Anton and Matej decided to leave and talk to the other refugees. Maybe someone will know how long they must stay in the field.

The women, young and older, watched the plump raindrops turn the fields into muddy land. Hannah said, "The distant field is now our bathroom. We'll have to walk through the soft, brown mud to get there now." The girls just nodded at the thought of nature's pleasant fields becoming their toilet.

A short time later, Anton and Matej returned to their

wagon. They were filled with the latest information on their current situation.

Matej said, "It is true. Families have been separated and the men have been put in slave labor camps." Hannah and Katica closed their eyes in sadness as they listened.

Anton was quick to add, "The Partisans are the group who are putting the men into slave labor."

Frightened, Katica said, "Anton, you and father made the right decision. As much as we love our country, Croatia, we can not go back!"

The metal wagon wheels rested in the often muddy fields for two long weeks. When heavy rain pelted the canopy fabric above, they rested on their feather bed under a hand-made down comforter.

Katica and Hannah wore the dark dresses and kerchiefs of war. White cotton was saved to make bandages. Mirjana and Maria being younger wore blouses and skirts. With serious eyes, they all watched the activity around them.

The British made a field kitchen near-by. A thin potato soup was the main meal.

As they lived in the same wagon, wore the same clothes, the days passed on. World War II was over – time to move the soldiers from the barracks. Weeks later– all the barrack buildings were emptied.

One sunlit morning, Anton announced, "The soldiers are gone. The British are moving us into the barracks."

"Will it be today, Father?" Maria asked.

"Yes, I think it will be," Anton said.

Time passed, several hours seemed like eternity to them. At last a British man came to them. "Come," he said, "make a place for your family." His words filled them with a flow of kindness.

Matej looked around at his family. He said, "It's not home but we are safe and together."

Anton and his family watched as several of the remaining British leaders walked among the weathered wagons. Hundreds of people heard similar words. An older man from a near-by wagon called to Anton. "I think it's time to go in."

Anton answered, "Yes, let's get our families inside the building. There should be at least a small area for all of us." The two men nodded in agreement.

Katica and Mirjana climbed down from their wagon home. They stared ahead with great intensity. Katica's eyes could almost bore a hole through the barrack walls. With slow, steady steps the family walked inside.

Anton and Matej took charge of their new situation. They walked with wide strides to a section near the bare walls where several bunk beds were stacked. Anton said, "Hurry, ladies, we must claim our beds. This looks like a good area."

Katica answered with great tenderness, "Yes, Anton, it is near the pot belly stove. We will feel some warmth on the cold days of winter."

Mirjana said, "I'm going back to the wagon and get our goose down comforters for the bunk beds."

"Me, too, I'm coming with you," said Maria. As the words left her lips, Mirjana's thoughts drifted back to the pleasant memories of making the comforters. First they plucked the white feathers from the geese. She remembered washing and slicing the feathers. Soon came the task of stuffing them into comforters or baby carriers.

Mirjana said, "Come now if you want to help me. Mother and Father will hold our spot."

"I'm coming Mirjana, please wait, you're walking too fast," said Maria.

"You're thinking of the past again. I know you," Mirjana stated.

"Just remembering how difficult it was to hold those geese still while we pulled their feathers," said Maria. The two sisters smiled at each other as their eyes met.

"Let's walk faster. We need to get our comforters and anything else we can carry," Mirjana said.

Soon their familiar wagon stood silent before them. Maria pulled the two soft comforters from the wagon and folded them to fit in her arms. Mirjana grabbed a few clothes and personal items. When they arrived back inside the barracks, they found Anton and Matej pacing back and forth across the worn floor boards.

"Girls, come here, we will make our bunk beds pleasant to rest and sleep on," Anton said.

Matej gathered his family together. "It is time for us to have a deep discussion about our life here," Matej said with firmness.

As the insecure family huddled together to talk and listen, they didn't know they were being watched. One British man, John, said to another, "What do you think about that family?"

The second man, Thomas, answered, "They can stay in that section. I believe they are Slavic people."

John spoke again. "We must keep the camp divided into sections by ethnic groups."

Thomas said, "John, don't be concerned. The Jewish Germans were sent to extermination camps. It is a fact, all Jews, the Polish, Russian and Hungarian Jews are in brutal death camps," Thomas empathized.

Both men looked downward. They found it impossible to comprehend the depth of cruelty that people could inflict on other people.

Unaware that they were being discussed and watched, Matej talked to his family. "The British don't know what to do with us. They don't have enough food and only have these barracks for us to live in. The once beautiful fields have become our toilets," Matej said.

Anton added, "It is difficult to believe but there are eight to twelve million people displaced in Central Europe."

Katica, always organized in her thinking, said, "Now I understand the masses of people, the transports and all the confusion."

Maria had another concern, "What will happen if one of us gets sick?"

"That is a good question," Hannah answered with the loving thought of being the mother and grandmother of the group.

Matej continued his talk. "Our meals will be prepared by the soup kitchen. The men will repair and do maintenance work on the buildings. There will also be a place for shoemakers and tailors. Others will maintain the grounds," he said.

Maria asked another question, "Will I go to school?"

Anton answered with a slight smile, "Yes, only here in the camp." He looked at Katica and said in a soft tone, "They aren't real teachers." Mirjana shrugged her shoulders, being older than Maria, she was bored with school.

"Mirjana, I have to tell you what I heard," Maria added.

"Go ahead, just tell me," Mirjana answered.

"The teachers will teach us by writing on a large blackboard. We will copy and write on small chalk boards with wooden edges. I saw them." Maria was pleased to tell the news about school.

****

Their sense of time vanished. The two to three thousand people in the camp were not allowed to leave. The only exception was a need of hospitalization.

Each day began with weak coffee and a slice of bread. Evening meals were often a thin potato soup made from rotting field potatoes that were brought to the camp.

During the long days, some of the men built out-houses which proved to be a slight improvement from the toilet fields. The foul smell lingered in their noses far too long.

Embarrassment became a frequent ordeal for the girls and women. They all shared a communal shower with twenty women once a week. In their section of the long building, Katica and Hannah stretched a clothesline and put a blanket over it for a small amount of privacy. The embarrassment was subdued yet long-lasting when a grandmother, mother and growing daughters saw each other naked. They always looked away with quickness yet their minds had already taken the sight in.

The days, weeks and months became a fog of mental duration. One day Mirjana had reached the end of her patience. "Maria, do you want to go outdoors, just outside the barracks?" Mirjana asked.

"Yes, of course, let's go now," said Maria.

Katica nodded yes, as she listened to her daughters. There was only a small amount of grass standing in the dirt. Maria noticed a few small stones.

"Mirjana, let's skip stones in the dry dirt," said Maria.

"Yes, mine will go farther than yours," challenged Mirjana. Stones were tossed, puffs of dry dust rose into the air.

"Wait, stop! I see something outside the fence," Maria said.

"I see it too. It's a small, furry rabbit," said Mirjana.

"I'm crawling under the fence to get the rabbit," Maria said with excitement.

Mirjana thought to herself how Maria was becoming bolder, stronger as time passed. With the life they lived, the weak did not always survive. Many of the strong were destined for death because of their beliefs or ethnicity. She wondered what would happen to them all.

Maria wiggled under the wire fence and snatched the soft bunny. "I've got it, Mirjana, help me get back," said Maria.

Success, they were both back. The two sisters stroked the soft bunny. They enjoyed a small slice of life for the first time in many months.

CHAPTER 11

WHISPERED SECRETS, TRAGIC ACTIONS

The proximity of many people crowded together in long buildings created raw emotions. There were small irritations such as the lack of space to walk and no place to go. The non-existence of privacy was constant. Dull, boring food followed with meal after meal of weak coffee and thin potato soup. At times, they enjoyed small mouthfuls of peas or beans. These irritations were lived each day. The deep secrets evolved over time.

By 1948, Anton was allowed to work outside of camp doing his usual job as a tailor. With his small wages, he managed to save enough earnings to purchase a wood stove. Just outside the barrack, the stove stood ready to cook food for their hungry family.

Hannah and Katica cooked on the stove while Mirjana and Maria carried small bundles of wood to keep it going.

They all shared the task of cleaning their stove. Handfuls of sandy dirt were scattered on top and rubbed in to remove food stains and little pieces of food debris.

The tense trial of ten families living together in one barrack sometimes stretched nerves to their breaking point. Mirjana's words erupted, "I've had enough of the public bathroom with no flushing allowed."

"Me too," agreed Maria. She added, "And all of us using the same pot during the long night is just too much!" Maria lashed out more, "It's just plain disgusting."

Katica and Hannah looked at them in complete agreement. Katica answered, "Your grandmother and I understand how you both are feeling. You know what bothers me the most?"

Both girls said, "What, Mother, what?"

Katica replied, "I can't tolerate being allowed to shower only once a week. Warming the water on the stove and hauling the heavy water to the shower is hard work."

After this heated talk, they all became silent. Thoughts of the passage of time drifted in their minds. They began their life in the barracks in 1945, years before.

Despite their words, despite their feelings, time dragged on as the family watched the barrack camp become more organized. The men continued to repair the barracks. The women worked in the fields where they harvested potatoes and planted juicy strawberries and tangy blueberries. Still other women planted seedlings which in time would become majestic forests. Much of the virgin trees had been destroyed by the war.

There were days when they released their pent-up

feelings but usually they were happy people. When the women spent days away from camp, they did not use poor, bad words to describe their living conditions. Their acceptance of being victims of war was heroic.

The days became weeks. The weeks passed into months. In the winter cold, white snow blew through the cracks of the wood walls. Mirjana and Maria, the two sisters of war, became closer and closer. They often sat together under their goose-down comforter as they compared their old life with their life of today.

Mirjana said to Maria, "I still can't get used to the cans. In one can we have to pee. If we go outside and are barefoot during the warm months, we have to step in another can to disinfect our feet."

Maria answered, "I know we shouldn't complain but sometimes it is just too much to bear!"

Mirjana spoke again. "Maria, I have to tell you. There is a new matter to deal with."

"Oh, no! What now?" said Maria.

Mirjana looked into Maria's eyes and glanced upward to her thick, black hair. "There's a lice breakout!" Mirjana said.

At that moment Katica walked towards them with yet another can in her hands. "Come girls. I'm going to dust you with this white powder and also spray your hair," she said. "Maybe it will keep the lice away from you."

"Wait," said Mirjana. "We need to find our kerchiefs." Their hands were quick to find them in the small pile of belongings.

Both girls closed their eyes as Katica dusted and sprayed them. Mirjana and Maria looked at each other in disbelief as they covered their beautiful, thick hair with the gray kerchiefs. Stray strands of white dusted hair escaped their head coverings. Grandmother Hannah spoke, "You need to wear the kerchiefs for one week."

As the family did their part to combat the lice, the men of the barracks worked together. A strong liquid was sprayed in every corner and under every bed. Life in the camp carried on.

****

While Hannah stayed close to Mirjana and Maria, Katica often wandered to talk with the other women. "Hello, Dora, how is your family doing today?" said Katica.

"Not well, I think my baby has an ear infection. He cries often and pulls at his ears," Dora responded.

Katica answered with concern. "You could do what some of the other young mothers have done. You are breastfeeding."

"You are right, Katica. With your support I'll do it," Dora said. With her crying baby in one arm, Dora used her other hand to lift her worn peasant-type blouse. Dora exposed her soft breast and placed it near the baby's ear. She squeezed her breast and released the warm breast milk into the baby's ear.

"Often breast milk cures ear infections. I have seen it happen. I hope it will be true with your baby," Katica said with encouragement.

Dora said, "Thank you," as her eyes filled with tears. "I miss my husband so much. He has never seen his child!

He fought in the war, came back and left again to find our families and relatives," Dora had continued.

"How long has your husband been lost?" asked Katica.

"A long time, you know how difficult it is to determine time here," said Dora.

"Yes, most of us seem to be in a mental fog regarding the passing of time in the camp," Katica answered.

"Oh, Katica, there is something more I need to talk to you about," said Dora.

"What is it Dora?" Katica asked. "We can talk now."

Dora began. "Here I am holding my baby who is almost twelve months. I am breastfeeding, creating a forever bond with my child. The same milk from within me nourishes him and may end his ear infection." Dora paused and continued, "All of this fills my thoughts, yet I hear their soft, whispered sentences. The words have an ominous sound to them!"

"Is it true Katica? You move around the camp more than I do. Your daughters, Mirjana and Maria, are older."

"Yes, Dora. It is true, not all mothers get to hold their babies." Katica's eyes glistened with tears. "There are a moderate number of infant deaths."

"Katica, are most of the baby deaths in our camp?" said Dora.

Katica knew the answer to Dora's question. "The infant deaths are not just in our camp. They happened in Croatia and in surrounding countries."

"Tell me more Katica, I need to know the truth," Dora said.

"We are living in difficult times. Most of the time, midwives deliver the babies," said Katica.

"The trained mid-wives do their best," Dora responded.

Katica continued, "Sometimes the mid-wives deliver babies who are deformed. At other times the babies' skin is blue tinged."

"Do the infants just die?" asked Dora.

Katica swallowed as she struggled to say the next few words. "Many are drowned in the small tub of water used for delivery." Both women fell into a deep abyss of black sadness.

Katica ended, "And no records were kept!" Dora and Katica squeezed each others hands. Katica walked the short distance back to her family's area.

****

Anton and Matej had just returned from their daily jobs. Hannah, Mirjana and Maria were making a small decision. Should they eat from the soup kitchen or try to cook something on their wood stove?

"You ladies decide on our meal. I have news," Anton said. They all turned to look and listen to him.

"The British say they have run this camp for about five years. They have completed their duties and the United Nations will take over," said Anton.

Mirjana spoke in a quick reply, "It seems like we have been here for a long time but I didn't think it was five years." They all nodded in agreement.

"United Nations people will be talking to us all tomorrow," Matej added.

Minutes later they ate scraps of old potatoes from the

fields and over-ripe fruit. The bunk beds felt especially small that dark cloud-filled night. With the early morning light, the family anticipated the visit and questions of the United Nations representatives.

Before an hour had passed, the camp became more alive. The United Nations people had arrived and the International Red Cross was with them. The good strangers walked among the refugees and seemed to be very interested in the children of all ages.

Mirjana raised her lovely head and stood tall as if to prove she was a young lady who survived. Maria's shyness took hold winning over her new maturity level. She cowered and kept near the back of her family.

One of the Red Cross ladies spoke, "Dear girl, come closer." With her arms stretched out, her eyes pleaded with Mirjana to join her! Katica nodded to Mirjana. With a hint of courage, Mirjana stepped forward.

"You are thin and I've noticed you coughing often," the Red Cross lady said.

Mirjana answered, "I eat what we have. There isn't always a lot. My cough started a few days ago." Her words tumbled out to the pleasant Red Cross lady.

"What is your name?" the Red Cross representative asked.

"I'm Mirjana. This is my sister Maria and my parents."

"Mirjana, I'd like to talk to your parents."

Mirjana took the verbal cue from the unknown Red Cross woman. "Maria, let's walk away for a little while," Mirjana said. The girls looked back as they walked with slow, heavy steps.

A concerned Maria asked, "What do you think they are talking about?"

"I don't know Maria. Please don't worry. Look they've stopped talking already," said Mirjana.

Maria and Mirjana hurried back to Katica and Anton. Mirjana could not get her words out fast enough. "Mother, Father, what did she say?"

Katica spoke first. "Mirjana, we have news for you. The International Red Cross has selected you to go with forty others to Switzerland."

"Switzerland? I don't understand," said Mirjana. She turned to her father with pleading eyes and no words.

"Mirjana, you are in your mid-teens. You need to attend a real school. You will be fine," Anton said. One by one, each family member hugged Mirjana.

Within days, Mirjana, the other children, and teens would leave for Switzerland. There was not much preparation for the "Fresh Air Program." Mirjana did not have many clothes to pack.

Katica understood Mirjana's thoughts. "I know you have some doubts, Mirjana, but the Red Cross wants your health to improve. They are concerned you are malnourished and so thin," Katica said with tenderness.

"I know I'm sickly but so are others my age and younger," said Mirjana.

"Remember, Mirjana, we all love you so much. This will be a good thing for you," Katica spoke with slow, careful words.

"But, Mother, I don't want to leave all of you," Mirjana's words caught in her throat.

As this unusual camp day wore on, Mirjana's thoughts drifted through the decision for her to go to Switzerland. She remembered being a young girl and sitting on a wood stool, watching her father cut the fabric with his heavy shears. Both girls had been fascinated by his work and amazed by the clothes he made. The war years had been filled with fear. The camp years were difficult, uncertain but not fearful.

Mirjana's high intelligence grew with her life-time experience of the harsh reality of war. Her beauty remained and her feisty side tried to stay calm just below her surface.

Maria still had a shy side but had blossomed with maturity and strength. She had difficulty with a touch of sorrow at the idea of Mirjana leaving them.

Mirjana's large, beautiful eyes closed slowly in thought only to open again and again.

As the long, camp day dragged into the blackness of night, Mirjana reached her conclusion. "Mother, Father," her voice strong, her eyes steady, "I'll be ready to leave for Switzerland in the morning."

Hours later, the morning dawned as Mirjana began a new adventure in her life. Matej and Hannah hugged their granddaughter as the others gathered around her. "Oma, Opa, I'll miss you both so much," Mirjana said.

Mirjana's dark eyes flashed at Maria. "You better tell me all about it when I see you again. I'll want to know every detail!" added Maria. Mirjana was her usual feisty self as she tried to masquerade her true feelings. She tossed her long, wavy black hair back and let it fall on her shoulders. With her nose tipped upward, she turned and walked away from her sister.

Only Katica and Anton were left to watch their Mirjana step onto the bus with the other children and teens. Many sad, concerned faces pressed against the window panes of the bus. All their good-byes were finished as the old bus rumbled along the rough road.

Sometimes Mirjana's outside demeanor appeared intelligent, yet fiery. Inside she was made of strength and depth. The bus ride provided her with time to reminisce. Her father had cut pieces of faded fabric from torn, old shirts to make children's clothing. The British threw away sweaters, hats and gloves. Her Grandmother had unraveled them all.

With great affection, Mirjana often called her, "Oma". During the camp days, this beloved grandmother used the retrieved yarn to teach Mirjana how to knit. Together they made stockings, hats, and old but new sweaters for them and others.

Mirjana's thoughts also slipped back to the deep embarrassment of seeing her mother and grandmother naked. There was no place to hide. They longed for some degree of privacy and more opportunity for cleanliness.

The vibrant green trees Mirjana saw pass outside the bus windows brought her back to the present. She had no idea that she would soon experience a major life change. Mirjana would live with a wonderful family for three months.

The warm, pleasant sunshine on Mirjana's face once again slipped her mind back to the camp. While Mirjana's parents worked, her grandparents kept close watch over her and Maria. Mirjana could still hear her grandmother's words, "Don't leave where you are; and, stay with your own people."

Mirjana's mental flash back in time continued. In the early camp days, not only Swabians but other nations remembered their war days of fear. The threat of abduction of the girls and women was always present.

In the barracks, Mirjana remembered how the German girls were fascinated with men of different ethnic backgrounds. Mirjana and Maria were not. They had another memory seared in their minds.

During their journey to the confinement camp, a suspected villain approached several of their wagons and shouted orders to them. "Get out and climb into the ditch by the road."

Great fear overtook them as they stumbled into the ditch. The man continued, "I brought my plane down but Hitler's men want me to prove myself to them." He raised his gun of death as they closed their eyes. With stiff hands of fear, they grabbed each others' hands. The loud gun shots shattered the air as the families stood rigid.

There was a slow realization of what had happened. Person after person, with hesitation, opened their eyes. They were alive! The pilot had shot at the road, not at the people in the ditch. Their bodies continued to tremble and shake as the ordeal happened. Mirjana knew she somehow needed to destroy these terrifying memories of war.

The old bus traveled many miles on its journey to Switzerland. It carried a precious group of children and teens of all ages. Mirjana's eyes grew heavy with sleep. The mental exhaustion of separation from her family took over. Mirjana's head rested on the back of her worn bus seat, within seconds she nodded in rest.

Miles behind in the confinement camp, Katica and Anton, Hannah and Matej thought only of their Mirjana. Katica spoke, "We know her life will be better there. When we start to miss her so much, we'll just have to remember she is well."

Hannah added, "There will be so much more for her to eat. I can still see Mirjana walking to the bus. Her legs were so thin ... like skin pulled over wooden spindles."

Maria brushed away a tear from her eye. "We will hear from her, I know," she said.

****

Mundane days in the camp wore on. Katica felt the need to wander and talk to her camp friend, Dora. Katica walked the familiar floor of the barrack building. In a short time Katica found her. "Dora, we haven't talked in awhile. Is there any word of your lost husband?" Katica asked.

"There has been no word of him for such a long time. I would like to tell you something. I hope you will understand," Dora said.

"What is it, Dora?" Katica asked with anxious words.

Dora looked down towards the floor and then locked her gaze with Katica's eyes. "I have become close friends with a man here. He wants me to marry him," Dora said.

With empathy, Katica said, "It is near impossible to know whether your husband is still alive after all this time."

"Oh, Katica, the deep anguish, the longing, the heartache is beyond explanation," Dora said. "It feels like I was in a deep pit of sadness with no bottom and no way to get out."

"And then this man offered words of comfort and strength. He became someone to share the mental and physical burden with," Katica responded.

"Yes, he did and he cared about my baby," Dora said.

"There is no need to feel guilty. War creates many different outcomes in people's lives," said Katica.

"We will be married soon. I will wear black like most war brides. There is still no white cotton or white fabric of any kind," Dora stated.

A few seconds passed while both women looked with gentleness at each other. Once again Dora spoke, "Another lady in camp found a black lace veil for me to wear. Come here in two days time for a short ceremony."

"I will be here for you," Katica answered. This exchange of words between two friends unleashed deep thoughts and emotions for Katica.

****

Matej and Hannah were walking among the other refugees as they searched for small amounts of extra food. Katica was alone in their small family space. Even Maria was away with her father.

The small bed seemed to call to Katica. She stretched

out on the bed and allowed all her buried secrets to rush to the surface of her mind. He had been so handsome and impressive. All the local young women had dreamt of being with him. The Manor House and the Nobleman who lived there created an irresistible allure. "Stop" - a silent scream flashed through Katica's mind.

At that moment, Maria returned from her walk. "Mother, your eyes look so troubled. What is wrong?" Maria asked.

Katica was quick to cover her true thoughts. With another real feeling, Katica answered, "I miss Mirjana so much!" Maria agreed, "We all do."

CHAPTER 12

QUIET DAYS – AWAITING THE DREAM

The atmosphere of the camp became subdued. The very air inside grew heavy with expectancy. What would come next? Each day the families waited for news or change. The ordeal dragged on for the hundreds of people still in confinement.

Anton was the usual one to hear news from the outside. His ears were always open when he worked as a tailor away from camp.

One sunlit afternoon he returned from work with hopeful news. Some people from another confinement camp had made an important decision. Their entire family would leave not only Austria but this part of the world. They struggled to make this choice but now were determined to accomplish the reality of it.

Anton said, "One of the young adults felt so much excitement about the family decision that he paced again and again across the worn, old floor until his parents said, 'You must relax Jakov, tomorrow we will start the process.'" Jakov's eyes shone and his face showed the hope he had buried inside for so many years. Anton finished the true story and looked at his family to see their reactions.

Katica's eyes revealed the depths of her thoughts. A deep secret, a significant part of her, remained in the small village in Croatia. Would she ever see the Manor House or who lived there again? Katica bit her lips in yet another attempt to keep her secret within her.

Hannah and Matej's faces reflected the same thought about leaving. They knew a life-changing decision needed to be made.

Maria's words leaped out of her mouth. "Father, did you say Jakov? I used to play with a boy named Jakov. He lived down the road where it curved to the West. We used to skip stones in the dirt when we were younger, before the war." Maria looked at her father for his answer.

"Yes, I'm sure the young man's name was Jakov," Anton replied.

"I wonder if it is the same person," Maria answered with a hint of a memory that surfaced in her mind.

With these new thoughts swirling through her head, Katica knew it was time to walk through the camp building. Weary, yet hopeful faces watched her pass. The large barracks felt very gray on this day. Was it the long time spent living here or was the pending decision clouding Katica's thoughts?

Soon she saw Dora who was sitting on the edge of her small bed. "Katica, come here, we must talk," Dora said. As Katica approached Dora she could see excitement dancing in her eyes. And yet the small muscles around her mouth betrayed another emotion – tension.

Katica spoke first. "Dora, your eyes are filled with joy but I see a tenseness around your lips."

"Oh, yes, Katica, I feel such a deep guilt about the marriage. Will you still come tomorrow to witness the ceremony?"

"Of course I'm coming and I do understand your feelings. You loved your husband very much. He has been gone so very long and the war is cruel," Katica answered.

Dora's eyes filled with tears. A large single tear found its way down Dora's cheek as she spoke softly to Katica, "I'll see you tomorrow." Katica carried the heavy emotional burden almost as much as Dora. The two friends of war parted with poignant feelings trapped within them.

Katica returned to her family and found them in deep discussion about their future. She looked at Maria and her parents as she spoke, "I'm overwhelmed with thoughts of Dora tonight. I just can't talk about the possibility of us leaving. Please excuse me while I try to sleep." Matej and Hannah nodded with understanding. Maria talked to Katica, "Mother, I would like to go with you in the morning. Dora needs support, not judgment."

Katica was proud of her daughter's wise words. She heard empathy and wisdom. A warm smile passed across Katica's face to her daughter.

Were Maria's words born from her survival of war, strength from enduring great loss or separation from her sister, Mirjana? Katica witnessed before her, how unusual events in life influenced and shaped the person each of us come to be.

Sleep was troubled for Katica that very dark night. She felt every inch of the small uncomfortable bed every hour until dawn.

As the first rays of light spread across the gray sky, Katica poured a cup of weak coffee. A few mouthfuls of stale bread once again became breakfast.

Maria joined her with eye-lids that did not want to stay open. "Mother, do you think Dora will go ahead with the wedding?" Maria asked.

"Yes, I think so. Dora is feeling such a complex set of emotions. She feels such a great loss with her first husband gone, lost and probably dead." The sound of the word - "dead" - made them both shiver.

Katica continued, "The emptiness Dora experiences is beyond our comprehension. The inability to touch and love another is one of our deepest needs." Maria looked into her mother's eyes as the bond between them melted together.

"Let's go to Dora," Maria struggled to say. Yet again they walked across the barracks. This time for a total different reason – a marriage at the end of war time.

As they approached, Katica and Maria saw Dora wearing a black lace kerchief and a simple gray dress. A small group of people gathered as a Reverend, far from his church, stood before Dora and her husband-to-be.

Katica and Dora exchanged small smiles just as the ceremony began. The Reverend stretched out his arms to include them all in the special event. His words drifted in the air around them. "The war has ended, it is time to begin our lives again," he spoke with facts and hope.

Dora and her new husband, Eric, stated their vows and made their promises. Under her happy exterior, something vague stirred inside Dora. It was a fast moving thought, almost a whisper, that she did not understand.

Within a short space of time, Katica, Maria and the others wished Dora and Eric happiness in the coming years. A young girl had picked a bouquet of colorful wildflowers. She placed the white daisies, yellow buttercups, and lavender in Dora's hands. This simple gesture became a cherished memory for the new couple who were beginning a marriage at the end of a major war.

Katica and Maria squeezed the couple's hands and gave long-lasting hugs. As mother and daughter walked back to their small area they knew the important decision they faced.

****

Matej and Hannah were deep in conversation. Wrinkles formed on Matej's forehead as he weighed the reasons to stay and the reasons to go.

Another refugee walked towards the family. He was pleased with the letter he held in his hand and presented it to Matej with a full smile. "Thank you, thank you so much," Matej said.

The letter came from Switzerland. The family was so eager to hear from Mirjana that Katica's fingers almost tore the letter open. Her hands trembled as she read their daughter's warm words to them all.

Mirjana wrote with emotion and stressed her life would never be the same again. "The Fresh Air Program" changed her life. She lived with a wonderful family for two months and would return to her real family in another month.

All the delicious, fresh food returned Mirjana to good health. Katica's eyes glistened with tears of joy and relief as she read her daughter's news.

There were times when Mirjana felt homesick. Her parents had placed a large German chocolate bar in her small suitcase. It was a complete mystery where and how they found the chocolate.

In the evening when she packed or unpacked her clothes, Mirjana said a German prayer and ate one small square of chocolate. That was the time when she missed and thought of her grandparents, parents, and Maria. Happiness mingled with sadness during her stay in Switzerland.

Mirjana ended her letter with these words, "Oma, Opa, the bathroom is inside the house. Remember when you watched Maria and I walk to the far end of the fields or hide in the woods? I really like the bathroom inside the family's house. See you in a few weeks time." A soft calmness settled over the family after reading Mirjana's letter.

****

The following morning Katica decided to visit and check on Dora and her new husband. As Katica stepped with caution around people sitting on the floor or brushed past the many small beds, she felt a strange yet strong sensation. The old walls of the confinement building seemed to breathe with a life of their own.

Within these walls, deep emotions had been felt. Piercing sadness had been endured. Lives were changed forever. The presence of the walls smothered Katica as she walked. She could feel each wall as it inhaled and exhaled with heavy breaths.

Katica coaxed her thoughts back to Dora and her husband as she approached their area. With disbelief Katica stared at the people before her. Dora's body shook as she cried without control. Her new husband lowered his head not knowing what to do.

Another man, who Katica did not know, stood near them with his body as rigid as stone. His eyes narrowed and his face contorted with disbelief and deep sorrow. The unknown man said, "Dora, I have been watching you from across the room. It looks like you replaced me."

The poignant feelings of three people poured out from their hearts. Dora felt guilt and sadness as she attempted to speak. "I thought you were killed. You had been gone so long..." Her words softened into silence. Dora could not look at her first husband, her real husband, or was he?

Dora ran to Katica and said, "What can I do? I'm being torn in two pieces."

Katica could not believe her eyes. The urgency, the depth of love and confusion cut the air between them like knives. War destroys people at every level of their being.

Lawrence, her first husband, shook his finger at Dora

and said, "How could you, we have a child together." His feet smashed into the floor as he left the stunned people behind him.

Dora's tear stained face and reddened eyes searched Katica's eyes. With a hint of mystery, Katica spoke with deep understanding. "This is heart wrenching for us all. Somehow we need to stay calm and think. I'm here for you." War brought these two women together in ways they never could have foretold.

Dora's sad life events raised another emotion. Often during times of crisis, people try to change or correct events. It is most difficult to accept that they have no control - often when they need it the most.

Katica hesitated as she walked away. After only a few slow steps she stopped and glanced over her shoulder. Dora watched as tears streamed down her cheeks. Both women nodded at each other.

The scars of war cut deep with many changes colliding around them. Would Dora and Katica ever see each other again?

Katica returned to Hannah, Matej, and Maria. She would tell them when the time was right.

****

At this very moment in time the Croatian family was on the edge, a black and white decision of their life time. Mirjana's letter had encouraged them. There were other countries where life was good — food, fresh and plentiful, freedom and opportunity existed.

Mirjana returned to the family from Switzerland with a flurry of hugs, kisses and hope. She was the catalyst for their imminent family decision. Hannah, Matej, Katica, Anton, Mirjana and Maria all sat together in their small confinement space.

Matej spoke first, "The war ended years ago and we're still trapped here in this camp."

Hannah said, "We can't go back to our Croatia. We heard of the violence and death of others who tried to return."

Mirjana joined in the important conversation, "We speak a dialect of German. People are not sure of us or what country we are from. We are second class citizens."

Hannah answered with an emphatic, "No citizenship has been granted to our people!"

Maria watched and listened as her father, Anton, slammed his fist on the small table. With firmness Anton said, "Our future here is dim. We must immigrate!"

Hannah and Katica's first reaction was to look at the girls. Their faces were still with the shock of reality. Mirjana spoke first, "We must do it!"

Maria said almost in a whisper, "Where will we go?"

Anton answered with a slight smile, "I think I know where Hannah and Katica want to live." Anton grabbed all their attention as they waited for his next words. "America, America is our dream!" he said with triumph.

CHAPTER 13

FROM YEARS OF FEAR
TO YEARS OF LOSS

The heavy, dark cloud of war lifted over them – only to be replaced by an endless gray sky. Time dragged on from the year 1945 to the year 1951. Long hours of thinking had rolled over layer upon layer in their minds. After all this mental exhaustion, the final decision to immigrate had happened within minutes. They waited to begin the immigration process with a great anticipation that was difficult to contain.

Camp life continued as a mundane existence for them all during this time of waiting. Matej worked on building upkeep and the outside grounds. Hannah's daily job was to work for the nearby farmers. She always said, "It's a job and the local farmers are good to us."

Katica left the camp by day to work at a Reforestation School. She said, "It feels good for my hands to work in the fresh, moist soil and grow tree seedlings." The lush, green land and golden plains were scarred – lost to war. The survivors planted small trees to re-create life and beauty across this region of Europe. Anton traveled the farthest from the camp. People in and near cities had the greatest need for a tailor.

Early one morning the first rays of daylight woke Katica. As she stretched her arms and attempted to keep her eyes open she heard everyone preparing for the routine of their day.

Katica's sleep had been troubled as she turned from one side and back over again. She must find Dora and talk to her.

With hesitation, Katica walked in the direction of the area where Dora should be. There was no Dora or either man who might be with her. A lady near her was smoothing a thin blanket on her bed. Katica asked, "Have you seen Dora?"

The older lady continued straightening her bedding without answering. People did not always know how to handle the sad situations around them.

Katica searched the building that she knew so well. In the far corner of the barracks, she saw Dora. Their eyes met as they ached to speak to each other. The two friends rushed to meet. Katica's hands reached out to grasp Dora's hands. "Let's step outside and walk around the building," Katica said.

"Yes, an older lady is holding my baby," Dora replied.

It was good for both women to walk in the fresh air; where before the stale, stagnate smell of gun fire and corpses used to linger. They both found these memories difficult to forget. Now the air had cleansed itself. It was a pleasure to take in deep, fragrant breaths.

The war was over, the emotional turmoil was not! "Dora, what happened the day after your wedding?" Katica's words blurted out.

With calm yet sad words Dora answered, "The very next morning, a representative of the Red Cross came just inside the door of the building."

All of us who were close enough to hear gathered near him. "Later today, a man is coming who is looking for his family. I wanted you to know," he said. He turned and left with the swift steps of a man with more messages to deliver.

Dora closed her eyes for a few moments. Her thoughts collided with raw tension. The man coming cannot be my Lawrence, not after all this time. The wedding had just happened.

"Sorry Katica, I was just re-living what happened," Dora said. She continued, "The Red Cross man came. Lawrence followed. There was a short confrontation between Lawrence and me. Lawrence stomped away with deep anger."

After a pause, Katica answered, "I'm so sorry Dora. It is almost impossible to believe that this could happen."

"I know," Dora said. "I'm in a state of complete loss. I don't know what to do."

"With time, patience and prayer you will do the right thing for you and your baby," Katica answered with tenderness. The two women parted, each carried the burden of an unknown future.

Katica returned to her own family. Each one, Hannah and Matej, Mirjana and Maria, and especially Anton waited to hear Dora's story.

Katica looked at their anxious faces. She began, "It's the war again, the hurt, the pain just won't stop." Katica's family leaned forward waiting for her next words.

"The man who the Red Cross predicted would be coming was Dora's first husband. There was a short, angry outburst from Lawrence," Katica said.

Silence filled the air. The youngest of the family spoke first. Maria, in her soft voice, asked, "Mother, what will Dora do?"

Katica searched all their eyes for their inner thoughts. Anton spoke, "We both should be at Dora's side. She will need to reconcile this sad series of events with first herself and then both men."

Mirjana said with fire in her words, "I hate war. Is it better to die first and fast or live on with other tragic events?"

Katica's strength showed in her clear words. "I know we have lived with death and violence beside us. I don't know what is worse, watching a loved one die or re-living in your mind what torture they could be enduring?"

Anton helped Katica as he added, "Despite it all, I know we are survivors. Also I heard there are consultants from other countries coming to camp during the next several days."

It was Mirjana who started the healing process. With a

deep gratitude for her three months of life in Switzerland, Mirjana felt the stirrings, the beginnings of a new life.

Maria had always admired Mirjana, her older sister. Mirjana was tall, beautiful with her long, wavy black hair. She had an intelligent, elegant way about her. Maria could not figure or understand all that made Mirjana who she was. Maria did know that she loved her sister very much.

In all ways the family loved both girls, but Maria somehow felt life in different ways than Mirjana. Once again the current situation showed the unique differences in the two young ladies.

As Katica lashed out at the war and the deep pain it still caused, Mirjana remembered that a good life could exist again. Mirjana's time in Switzerland made her determination, her will to survive, an impressive strength never to be denied. Mirjana would not let this war destroy her, the family or her people. Switzerland had nurtured what already existed in Mirjana. She had healed on several levels, the physical, the emotional and the spiritual.

Mirjana turned to Katica, "You have every reason to be angry but right now we have to be ready for the consultants who are coming."

Anton took over the serious conversation. "I'm not sure which countries are coming with representatives," he said. "We have completed our paperwork."

The following morning there was no soft hush of words as everyone prepared for their daily routine of camp life. Excitement and lively, loud sentences raced around the building. The family dressed, ate their small meal and waited for the first consultants to arrive.

Mirjana touched the red, crocheted edging of her peasant type blouse. With her second hand, Mirjana's long fingers passed through her silky, dark hair. Her thoughts returned to Croatia where the women crocheted bright edging on blouses. That time of their life in Croatia was gone forever.

Mirjana's thoughts were broken with Maria's words. "They are here, right now. Come on, we must listen!"

Most people hurried to get close to the consultants. Many felt hope that this was the beginning of a good, new life. Others were reluctant to hear how the ordeal of immigration took place. Anton and Katica watched the very different reactions of people.

Mirjana voiced her thoughts first. "People should know that hope was the force that made us survive. We should never lose it."

Maria replied, "Yes, you are right, but hope is an apparition. Sometimes it is bright and shines. You feel life will be better." Maria looked downward.

Anton added, "At other times the hope apparition turns dark with jagged, rough edges."

"And it vanishes, gone," Katica said. "It's understandable people are unsure of what to do right now."

Three consultants from foreign countries stood before the people. The men looked out at the mass of humanity and knew the importance of their job.

The first spoke, "I'm from Australia. Those of you who want to come to Australia bring your family and papers to me." With a mix of hesitation and hope several families approached him. The soon-to-be immigrants clutched their papers in their tight hands.

The second representative came from a land so far away that it was difficult for the camp people to comprehend the distance. His words had an unusual accent but they could understand him. "I will take some of you with me to Argentina. Please form a line here in front of me." Fathers looked at Mothers. Brothers and sisters stared into each others faces. Uncertainty covered their eyes but some still stepped forward.

A proud man, the last of the day, offered his words, "I give you peace and rest in my country of Canada." His optimism was infectious. Many families rushed to him.

And then it was over...... The powerful attempt to immigrate had failed.

Mirjana and Maria grabbed each other's hands. Katica and Anton turned with one abrupt movement and walked back to their small familiar area. The family followed without a clear comprehension of what had just happened.

As Mirjana and Maria walked with their hands clasped together, Katica did not realize what was happening behind her. Her friend, Dora, was living several minutes of her own drama.

****

Dora could not grasp the fact, the reality, that Lawrence, her first husband, had found her and their baby. With an intense reaction of anger at his discovery, Lawrence had walked away. Lawrence's interpretation was betrayal by

Dora. With his impulsive desire to abandon Dora and their child, Lawrence left behind immense, deep hurt to the point of emotional pain.

Eric, the new husband, had watched the scene unfold before his eyes. Disbelief, sadness and even guilt churned in his mind. Eric stood at the far edges of the area. He wanted to wrap his arms around Dora and support her. Another part of Eric knew he had to allow Dora to filter all of this through the most inner part of her heart.

Dora stopped her thoughts and called out to the consultants as they each began the endless paper work before them. "As you traveled to the different camps did you ever see or hear of a man named Lawrence?" Dora added, "He was very loud and strong-willed as he searched for his family."

"No," the man from Argentina said. "I always try to remember the ones suffering the most from loss and separation."

The representative of Australia looked up. "Most are enduring such deep pain of loss and others are lost in grief. The spirited ones, it is difficult to forget their faces. Sorry, I didn't see him."

The kind, proud man from Canada overheard Dora's pleading words. "Wait until I finish this family's paperwork," he said.

A long several moments later the Canadian spoke. "I believe I saw and heard your Lawrence. Was he a large man with dark hair and eyes?"

"Yes," Dora said. "Tell me more."

"He was full of anger. It overtook his sadness. He talked of losing his wife and child to another man."

"It had been so many years. I feared he was gone. I had to go on for my child and myself." Dora's eyes brimmed with tears.

"He ranted on to everyone he met. He finally said he was going to the most distant forest place he could find and try to forget," the Canadian consultant finished.

"Thank you for your honesty. At the very least, it gives me some closure," she answered with a small gratitude shrouded in sadness.

Dora quickened her steps to catch up with the Croatian family she knew the best. "Katica, Katica, wait, wait for me."

Everyone turned around to listen as Dora poured out her story. Not only their eyes but their hearts were riveted on Dora.

Katica spoke with great wisdom. "Lawrence has not found the ability to empathize."

Dora stared at Katica in complete silence. Katica continued with tenderness, "Dora, you must search your heart for the forgiveness Lawrence needs for leaving." The entire event was another deep scar of war.

Maria looked up at her mother with respect for how she absorbed Dora's plight. Maria had to add her own thoughts to the poignant scene that had just played out. "Why don't people learn from the horrors of war? They just keep fighting more and more wars!"

Anton responded, "Through all the ages of time people

have placed self-interest, greed and power above love for others." Anton simmered with an inner anger.

****

Evening settled in around them. They processed all that had happened. Dora would come to forgive Lawrence and herself. She had a baby to love. Perhaps with time and slowness, Eric would come back into her life. Lawrence was gone forever! In this slice of time, Eric kept fading into the shadow places of the camp.

The disappointment of the international consultants weighed heavily on the entire family. So few countries had come forward to accept them.

It had all happened in a rapid passage of time before them. "Father, Mother," Mirjana said. "It was like watching a play filled with drama but we couldn't jump in to be part of it." Everyone nodded their heads in complete agreement.

"No one came from the country we wanted, the United States of America," Katica said.

Anton added, "We have no Marriage or Baptismal Records. I'm afraid that will work against us."

They listened as Mirjana said, "I overheard several men talking. Their conversation was about the United States limiting Germans. We have no official documents."

"Listen, you all must listen. We are stateless with no citizenship, but we are displaced people with a dream," Anton spoke with authority and love.

CHAPTER 14

THE SHIP OF TIMELESS DREAMS

The entire family felt limp with emotional exhaustion. After years of confinement camp living they had heard the exciting news that several more countries were coming to offer them a new life in a new land.

Their high spirits had dropped when the quota numbers had filled for the countries offering new homes over the past several months and years. As another ordinary morning dawned, Katica spoke to Anton, "Since some families have left there is a different feeling here."

Anton answered, "I know, I feel it too. It's difficult to describe."

Katica's eyes rested on her entire family around her. There was Matej and Hannah, Anton and the two daughters who she loved with all her being. Katica said, "I think we are all moving in slow motion!"

Mirjana's thoughts floated in her head. She had been

about ten years old when they came to camp. By 1948 she was allowed to attend the Austrian, all girl, school.

Even though Mirjana and the other girls from camp spoke German with a dialect from Croatia, the Austrians did not see them as Germans. They were second class citizens. Again Mirjana felt the pain of no citizenship granted to her people.

Mirjana came out of her silent thoughts. She almost shouted, "Come Maria, we must start our forty-five minute walk to school."

Maria turned and looked at her mother. "How much longer do we have to walk so far to go to school?"

Katica patted Maria on the shoulder. "Keep hoping the American Consul comes to camp."

Maria answered, "I will keep thinking of America, Mama." As the girls left for school Maria just had to say one more thing. "Besides the long walk, Mirjana always does better on the tests at school. It just isn't fair."

As the girls trudged along the road to school, Mirjana showed a small book of blank pages to Maria. "Look, Maria, Mother gave this book to us to have our friends sign their names," Mirjana said.

"Mother is thinking ahead and giving us hope too," Maria answered.

That afternoon when the girls returned to camp they heard exciting news. "Mirjana, Maria, the American Consulate is close by us. They might be coming to our camp."

Mirjana and Maria looked at each other and smiled. They had asked many friends to sign their book today.

The names of their friends had begun to fill the empty pages. The next day they would try to get more names and favorite memories. Maybe the girls would be taking the small book of names to America after all.

Anton gathered his family around. "I know we have been very disappointed in the past. Countries have come and countries have gone," he said. "We will have another chance soon."

Katica added, "I know we have been through this ordeal before. We started the process, all the paperwork in 1948. Now it is near the end of 1951 and we are still here. Somehow our patience has endured."

Mirjana's loud words released her emotions. "It has been more than three years of fearing rejection, countries filling their quotas and no consul from America."

Anton tapped his fingers on the small wood table near him as he waited with slight impatience to speak. "We all have experienced raw fears, devastating disappointments and years of confinement living." The family listened and watched his face. Anton began again, "I have exciting news. The American Consul is coming tomorrow! It is a fact now."

Excitement and hope raced through them like an electrical current. Everything could now change. America was coming!

The night seemed endless as hours crept by. As the first rays of sunlight spread across the land, they woke filled with anticipation of today's visit. One more breakfast of stale bread and weak coffee was swallowed.

Anton and Matej reviewed their paper work again

and again. Katica and Hannah encouraged the men to follow them to the center of the large camp room. Mirjana grabbed Maria's hand. "Come, Maria, come. Today could be the day," Mirjana said with a high spirit in her voice.

They stood huddled together as they waited for the cracked camp door to open. At last the door creaked as it moved and the American Consul walked in. He worked his way through the mass of people to the center of the building.

The American tried to conceal his feelings as he saw the thin faces of the refugees. Some looked almost haggard to him. He extended his arms and opened them in a large gesture of welcome.

It was at this moment in time the American Consul spoke with authority. He began, "The year is 1951 and the United States has reached an important decision. We would like our country to become your country. America wants to give many of you a home forever."

A movement of people rushed toward him. The family held on to each other and managed to reach his writing table. The only thought Mirjana could hold in her head was the reality – they stood before the American.

Lines of worry were etched across Anton's face as he released the Austrian documentation papers from his tight fingers. The family watched in silence as the American reviewed their information. Tension grew stronger as he read one paper and checked it with another.

At last he raised his eyes and looked at each of their anxious faces. "Your family is accepted. We will make the travel arrangements for the train to take you to

Bremerhaven. One of our ships will take you to America," he said with kindness.

A river of joy flowed over the tense family. The most important adventure of their lives was about to begin. In a state of sheer excitement they packed their few belongings.

A second rush of thoughts filled their hearts and minds. Anton and Matej became the proud fathers who would travel with their families to the land of their dreams. Mirjana and Maria's joy spilled out of them. Mirjana would often blurt out, "I just can't wait another hour. We're finally going to America."

Katica's face shone with happiness for her family. Her mother, Hannah, noticed something more going through Katica's thoughts. Katica tried to hide the secret. She feared her own eyes would betray her.

As Katica's family and the other fortunate ones prepared for the long trip, Katica longed for seclusion. A part of her needed the deep silence of solitude.

America proved to be a country of action. Within a few days they took the train ride to the seaport of Bremerhaven. With only a slow look over their shoulders, Katica and Anton had absorbed their last look at the confinement camp which claimed several years of their lives. Camp was gone forever as they rode a train to freedom.

It rumbled along forty miles of tracks near the River Weser. The cold, deep water of the North Sea awaited them.

"Oma, Oma, look at the huge ship," Maria shouted with amazement.

A warm smile came to Hannah's face. She had not been called "Oma" for a long time. It was her beloved name used by her granddaughters before the war shrouded their world.

Hannah and Katica stared at the large transport ship that rested on the deep, blue waves of the North Sea. "Soon we will be on a ship like that," Anton said. "All of us together sailing to the United States."

As they cherished the scene before them, a man entered the train and gave instructions. "You all must proceed on to the holding camp," he said in an efficient voice.

The sound of the word "camp" subdued their feeling. "Not another camp, we can't do it!" Maria shouted. The air around them crackled with empathy for each other.

Time became a blur as they left the train and made their way to the holding camp, one sluggish footstep after another. For the following two, long weeks, the family learned what a holding camp was. It was a place of constant and thorough checking. The women and girls experienced physical exams. Their faces blushed pink when they realized the Americans were searching them for all kinds of diseases. The older women really understood. It was an interesting fact that the men did not have to be checked.

After two weeks of holding camp, the transport ship floated into Bremerhaven's deep port. The military ship, the USS General Hersey, would carry them over rough seas to America.

The family fell into a light sleep of changing positions

and memories laced with recent events and deeper thoughts. They were not rested with the first morning light.

In a state of complete excitement, they boarded the USS General Hersey up the steel steps and onto the ship. The date of December 12, 1951 would never be erased from their minds. At sixteen years of age, Mirjana felt an indelible mark on her young heart that could never be released! They stood on the deck of a huge ship that would cross the vast ocean to America.

Maria giggled as she said, "Mirjana, my legs feel wobbly on this ship."

"Me, too. Look Maria, we are slowly moving away from the seaport," Mirjana answered.

All their faces shone with an indescribable joy. Their eyes were mesmerized by the green, blue water of the North Sea. The watery arm of the Atlantic led to the full expanse of sea where the ocean met the horizon. This Croatian family began their journey.

Only Katica had a distant look in her eyes. Her unusual mood was broken by instructions. A middle-aged American man spoke in loud words. "There are a thousand refugees on this ship. We need to have rules to prevent chaos." Most people looked at each other with an understanding of his words.

The American began again, "Men and women will have separate sleeping quarters. Mess Hall will be a strict daily regimen." In a couple of hours the family would experience the true Mess Hall.

Military guards walked among the refugees. Mirjana

and Maria listened with fascination as they heard the different languages spoken by the guards. An inquisitive guard approached Katica. "Is your family hungry?" he asked.

The girls wanted to shout, "We're starved!" Instead they used timid words. Mirjana was glad she learned English at the Austrian school.

The guard led them to the Mess Hall and sent them inside. Rows of long tables filled the room. Anton was the first to speak. "I hope there is more food for us, but look everyone is standing to eat."

They moved with the crowd and found themselves in a long line waiting for dinner plates of food. With full plates in their hands, they managed to find six places together to stand and eat.

This was only the beginning of the Mess Hall adventure. Maria and Mirjana's beautiful eyes grew wide. As the girls placed their dinner plates on the long, metal table, there was immediate movement. The plates rolled away!

Maria and Mirjana grabbed for their plates. Hannah and Matej, Katica and Anton found themselves doing a frantic reach also. Plenty of food at last and there it goes. The family sighed with relief as they watched the plates hit raised edges all around the long tables! Someone in the ship-building industry had found a way to prevent food from falling to the floor. The strength of the ocean waves could even be felt in the Mess Hall below deck. Katica spoke for them all. "That was the most unique way we have ever eaten!" They all nodded in agreement. Maria could not stay silent, "I want to do it again!"

After eating they returned to the deck to explore the large ship. High winds whipped around them while the ship rolled over the powerful waves. An endless wall of green, frothy water rushed towards them and their ship. They were in awe of the ocean!

Time seemed non-existent as they stood on deck absorbed in the sight, the sound and even the smell. Katica and Hannah were thrilled by the endless sparkling water as it captured the sun's rays. Anton and Matej attempted to understand the depth of the ocean and the distance they would travel.

Maria said, "I like the smell. Even the air smells salty when you breathe it in."

Mirjana watched as the mighty waves slammed into their ship. It climbed up the front wall of water and plunged down the back side of the waves. The motion, the movement happened again and again. She spoke with soft, difficult words, "I'm going to be sick. Mother, help me."

Katica raced to a pile of paper bags she had noticed earlier and grabbed several. She reached Mirjana who was holding her stomach and closing her eyes. Seconds later Mirjana vomited into one of the brown, paper bags. The beauty of the sea transformed into a wrenching spell of sea sickness.

Evening approached with the men and women separating for sleep. Hannah took the girls to the area below the deck. Mirjana and Maria chose the bunk beds on the bottom. "Yes, girls, the lower beds should be safe for you," Hannah spoke to them.

As they crawled under the cozy blanket on their beds, Mirjana clutched a handful of clean, paper bags. She silently hoped she would not need them during the night.

Maria asked Hannah, "Where is mother?"

Hannah replied, "She wanted to stay on deck. There are many thoughts, like heavy boulders, she has pushed to the depths of her mind."

With those deep words Maria looked away to concentrate on their sleeping arrangement for the first night on the ocean vessel. Bunk beds, full stomachs and a softer almost smooth motion lulled Mirjana and Maria into a deep sleep.

****

On deck, Katica's eyes searched the blackness of night on the deep ocean. It was endless and intense with the sky above and the water beneath. The great dark sky had swallowed most of the stars. Only a small cluster glistened and sparkled just above her head.

Those few stars seemed to beckon her and called to Katica from across the universe. Croatia and the Manor House were left behind on a now distant shore. A precious memory from Katica's soul and heart drifted to the surface. There had been love between a young lady who brought fresh churned butter and a nobleman who lived in the large, stone Manor House!

Katica was beautiful with unforgettable eyes and long, dark wavy hair. The aristocrat was impressive, tall with handsome, masculine features. His strong face was framed with dark, red hair with slight streaks of blonde.

It was a forbidden love with stolen minutes of affection that grew into love. The longing to see each other perhaps once a week expanded with time.

The clash between their paths in life was clear from the beginning, the village girl and the nobleman. In time, strong passion took control.

For two months, Katica avoided the stately Manor House and the man who lived there. At last she was forced to go.

She arrived with warm butter in her pottery bowl and placed it on the fine carved wood table. He came behind her and stroked her soft hair.

Katica turned with slow, careful movement. Their eyes met and locked together with a deep bond. He said, with great tenderness, "I have guessed why you have not come for so long."

Katica answered, "You are right, what shall we do?"

"I have thought a long time about this happening. With deepest regret, I give you my child as a gift!" With his eyes lowered, a single tear fell from the nobleman's eye.

With sadness and empathy, Katica responded, "I understand and expected your decision. You will always be in my memory."

"Go now, my love, stay strong and healthy. You and our child will go on forever with me also." He hugged Katica, turned and walked away down the long hallway.

****

A powerful wave crashed into the ship and forced Katica's thoughts to return to the present. She must go to her mother and daughters. The burning memories of her life must rest now.

CHAPTER 15

THE SEA FOAM TRAIL

Daybreak approached on the azure water, as the ocean reflected the rising sun. Anton and Matej were already on deck, breathless with the sight before their eyes.

Below deck, Mirjana and Maria woke with the same, quick thought. Mirjana spoke first, "We really are on an ocean liner, do you believe it, Maria?"

"Mother, Oma, wake up, we must go to the Mess Hall and up on deck," Maria said with excitement in her voice.

Katica rubbed sleep from her eyes and replied, "Yes, let's get ready. There's food waiting for us."

Within minutes they walked to the Mess Hall and found a place in line. This time they enjoyed their food and were not surprised when the plates moved away from their eager forks and spoons.

"Let's go, girls. There's fresh air on deck and plenty to see, I'm sure," Katica said.

As they climbed the strong steel steps and stepped on

deck Hannah remarked, "The sunshine feels so good and the air is fresh."

Mirjana spoke, "Come on, there is something happening on the far end of the deck."

Soon they saw the ship's crew with large buckets in their hands. Maria said, "Something smells terrible. Oh, it's awful."

It soon became obvious what the men were doing. Heavy bucket, after bucket filled with the foul stink of raw garbage was thrown overboard. Katica and Hannah rolled their eyes at each other as Mirjana looked around for paper bags.

Anton came up behind them and watched their reaction. "Good morning ladies. I know what you are thinking but what else can the crew do with all the garbage?"

Even Matej placed his arm against his nose to block the stench. "We shouldn't walk away too soon. The waves are changing," said Katica.

Maria called out, "Look, everyone, there are giant whales coming!"

Huge black whales followed the ship as they sensed the rancid trash. Soon all the garbage that floated on the waves or below the surface was devoured by the whales' powerful jaws. Everyone watched in amazement at the ocean spectacle before them.

The whales broke apart the ocean waters as they surfaced and gulped air. More garbage was sucked into their throats.

As she watched the whales, Mirjana felt it swell in her stomach. Her seasickness returned with relentless vomiting. The paper bags became her unwanted friends during the long journey as complete exhaustion overtook every muscle in her thin body.

When night time came Mirjana longed for her bunk bed. Only sleep gave her a reprieve from the endless nausea.

The USS General Hersey seemed like a speck of sand on the vastness of the night ocean. Both large, white moon and sparkling stars disappeared on this particular night.

****

Without warning, the deafening sound of war planes thundered toward their ship! The noise ignited instant fear in Katica! She bolted out of bed.

Katica screamed, "The planes are coming. They will drop bombs on the ship!"

Anton, in an instant, was at Katica's side. "Katica, everyone is safe. You had a nightmare," Anton told her with great tenderness in his voice. He held her close with a strong hug.

In her fear and confusion, Katica asked, "Are you sure? Anton, where were you? You came so quickly."

"I was on deck, close to the stairs that led to your sleeping area. I would know your scream wherever I heard it," Anton answered.

"I know you would recognize my scream, I know." Katica closed her eyes for a few seconds as she reached for Anton. "You are always here for me. I can feel your love."

Anton calmed Katica and waited for her to fall back to

sleep in her ship's bunk bed. It was only at this time that his mind cleared. In silent words he thought, "I need to leave here right away. I'm not supposed to be here." Anton raced to the men's section of the ship.

****

The next day after Katica's nightmare, forced the entire family to confront their present life. They must put their war fears behind them, in their turbulent past.

Once again on deck, they focused on the beauty of the deep blue ocean. The water sparkled in the sunshine. Maria held her arm out toward the edge of the ship's deck. "I wish I could feel the sea spray, but I can't, the ship is way too tall," she remarked with a sigh. Everyone smiled at her.

The days fell into a pattern of life at sea. Time on deck was fresh air, sunshine and foggy mist. The constant roll of ocean waves was a thrill for some, while others felt a wave of their own – nausea.

Mess Hall provided a dependable source of food once they learned to hold on to their plates. Mirjana's fight against seasickness hindered her from eating large amounts of her meals.

The smooth black whales continued to follow the path of garbage as the USS General Hersey plunged through the waters towards North America.

One particular night, a full week after the departure from Bremerhaven, all of the family decided to sleep early, except for Katica. Hannah glanced over her shoulder as she looked at Katica with deep concern.

"Go ahead, girls, with your grandmother. I'll come below deck soon," Katica told Mirjana and Maria. Anton and Matej understood Katica's desire for solitude.

****

When they all left her behind, Katica stared at the endless depths of darkness of the night sky above the ocean. Katica felt a connection with the universe in this moment – the night became sacred.

Her mind traveled back through time to Croatia, to the Manor House, to the nobleman. The gift of a baby was given to Katica by a man of the aristocracy.

His decision, a burden of inherited wealth and upper class, caused intense pain to dwell within him. Katica carried within her a life created by love, but plagued by current perceptions and rules.

The thick darkness of this particular night became even more sacred as it drew her back into the past. In the depths of her sadness so many years before, Katica had approached her parents. She felt the urgency to tell her story to Matej and Hannah.

They had listened with deep concern and moist eyes as they felt their daughter's pain. From the simple task of delivering sweet, fresh churned butter, to the slow process of a forbidden love, to the conception of a tiny embryo – the truth was revealed.

Matej and Hannah were shocked into silence. The three held the secret in their hearts as they attempted to live each day with the challenge ahead of them.

Katica remembered she took the lead with the strong support of her parents. As it became obvious to the villagers that she carried life within her, the three thought only of the baby. The health of Katica and her child were the only matter of importance.

Katica's memories continued to consume her. As the months passed, she no longer took the fresh butter to the Manor House. The emotional pain would have been too much to bear.

One stormy night, it happened! With an instinctive motion, her hand had pressed against the small round area of her abdomen in her pregnancy. It was the eighth month of Katica's pregnancy when intense pain ripped through her. The bleeding started as she called out to Hannah, "Mother, hurry, get the midwife."

She had rested on her bed, eyes closed, as she waited. Fear gripped Katica as she felt more blood released.

In a short time she heard her mother rush in with the midwife. Though short of breath herself, she began her work. Within minutes Katica saw a look of horror on her mother's face.

Katica hadn't waited for the midwife to say, "Push." The urge to push happened during her short memory lapses. The midwife almost screamed, "Now, push now!"

The passage of the baby was the most severe pain she had ever experienced and then came absolute silence. Her blue tinged baby was cradled in the midwife's arms. Katica reached over and stroked her little soft cheek, still wet from being inside her.

Katica's eyes locked into the eyes of the midwife as they

stared at the umbilical cord wrapped around her baby's neck. The cord of life had become the cord of death!

The three of them, Katica, Matej, and Hannah, alone suffered deep, emotional pain. Few words were spoken for two days in their house of silence until Katica heard a knock on the back door. When she opened the door she saw a stranger with his head bowed. He spoke only two soft words, "I'm sorry." His hands held a small wood casket.

Katica helped Hannah and Matej place her baby in the brown box. They wrapped her in Matej's finest silk suit lining material.

As Katica looked at her for the final time, she was struck with the beauty of her baby. Her nobility would have been obvious to all who saw her. Katica was overwhelmed by her thick bright red hair. Croatians hair was dark brown or black, never red. Was it the ocean mist or Katica's eyes crying again as she was flooded with her memories?

****

Somehow, Katica found her bed that powerful night. She didn't remember falling asleep.

Katica woke the following morning with an urgent thought. She must find Anton. This strong, sensitive man came to her in the small Croatian village months after whispered words echoed around her.

Anton had said, "I have watched you, longed for you and loved you for a long time."

Katica remembered being stunned by his words. Anton spoke again, "Let me heal you and take care of you. It is time."

She remembered how she melted with Anton's words. Love began to grow between them. Anton knew her past as he placed empathy first.

Several large waves slapped the sides of the ship. The abrupt sound crashed into her thoughts as it ended her memories for now. Katica stared at the white sea foam trail as their ship cut through the cold, dark water. As the sea foam was left behind, should she try to leave her past behind?

CHAPTER 16

COME, COME
TO AMERICA

This Croatian family, bruised by war, rode the mighty waves of the Atlantic Ocean. About a week into their journey, they decided to linger over their Mess Hall meal. It seemed like a good time to talk.

Mirjana stared at the small piles of food on her plate. "If only I could eat, the motion from the rolling waves keeps giving nausea to me," she said.

"Oh, Mirjana," Maria said. "Remember when we put bread chunks in the chicory coffee?"

"Yes, Maria, I do remember. It didn't taste good but it was actual food in our stomachs. I guess it was something like comfort food to us," Mirjana answered.

A soft, knowing look came into Mirjana's eyes as she looked at them all. "Oma didn't eat all of her slice of bread in the evening. She saved small pieces for Maria and me."

Grandmother Hannah closed her eyes for a few

seconds. She responded, "How could I eat all my bread when I saw my two granddaughters so hungry?"

Anton added, "Don't talk about the camp food. All I remember is no meat sandwiches. We only ate lard, spread on bread. It was difficult to swallow."

Matej joined in the conversation. "Forget the food. The bitter cold is something I can't forget. Remember the snow in the cracks of the barrack walls?"

"It was freezing cold, yes, actual snow in the walls. Seeing it made us feel even colder," said Maria.

Mirjana's turn came, "There was something more that really bothered me in the confinement camp. The fence around the buildings made me feel so closed in."

Katica talked softly to her daughter. "I'm so sorry you experienced that deep feeling of no escape, no freedom."

Mirjana spoke again, "The history of our Croatian people, we were nomads; to be held captive in one area was not something that flowed through our arteries and veins."

Hannah asked, "Is there more, Mirjana?"

Mirjana answered her grandmother. "I felt smothered. I wanted to escape to another place through the pages of a book. There were no books in the camp!"

With great respect, Hannah said, "There was one book – the Bible." Everyone looked at her with their own deep thoughts.

The discussion could have continued but too many yawns were sneaking across their faces. They separated to male and female quarters where the sea rocked the family to sleep.

The sun's rays or misty fog surrounded the military transport ship each morning. Day after day the USS General Hersey sliced through the deep waters of the Atlantic as she headed for the harbor of New York City. The excitement of the people on board started to build. Everyone started counting the days.

On December 12th, 1951 their ship had left Bremerhaven seaport. Two weeks later, they sailed into New York! It must have been part of a Divine Grand Plan – it was Christmas Eve in America.

Joy overtook their exhaustion. Wide-eyed, they could not describe what they were feeling. No words flowed from their mouths.

The ship now floated on gentle waves as they passed the Statue of Liberty. Katica's words broke the awe-struck silence. "I can feel freedom and liberty in the air. It surrounds us like a protective cocoon."

Mirjana looked at her family and everyone around her. "I want to get off the ship and kiss the ground." People nodded, smiled and raised their arms in cheers!

They sailed closer and closer to Lady Liberty. The proud statue stood one hundred fifty one feet high. She was created from sheets of copper sculpted over the sturdy steel framework. They not only felt the potency of freedom in the air, they experienced the symbol before them, their eyes brimmed with tears.

The family absorbed all that surrounded them as a crew member stepped forward. He began, "Yes, you have arrived in America, but there is something I have to tell you."

Every person on the deck riveted their attention to him. A thin, gray-haired man shouted, "Tell us, tell us now."

One of the sailors who brought them to America said, "It is Christmas Eve in the United States. There are not many people working. You will have to sleep on the ship for a few more nights."

It was only a small disappointment for all the war refugees on board the USS General Hersey. With a combination of emotional excitement and physical exhaustion, the weary group found their small beds.

During the overnight hours, a small number of Americans patrolled the ship. They walked with slow, careful steps among the people who had come from distant countries at the end of war.

A slow creeping sun brought early rays of sunshine to the dark, blue water surrounding the ship. Mirjana rubbed sleep from her eyes when she noticed something on her pillow. "Maria, wake up, come on, wake up. There is something on our pillows," Mirjana said.

"What do you want? I'm still tired," Maria managed to answer.

Both girls picked up the "something" on their pillows. Their hands touched the smooth, yellow long object. It felt firm but soft on the inside.

Katica smiled at them. "Peel it and take a bite off the top," she said.

Mirjana and Maria were hesitant but did what she said. Inside it was white and tasted delicious. Both girls spoke at the same time, "What is it?"

"It's a fruit called a banana," Katica answered with

happiness as she watched her daughters experience the taste of their first banana.

The family's joy mingled with anxiety as a long table was set up. They feared there would be some reason that the people would not be allowed off the ship.

Anton was quick to calm his family, "Our paperwork has been done on the ship and we are processed."

They approached the table with the German speaking immigration officer. In the German language they answered "yes" or "no" to his questions. Only one more night on their rescue ship – they were accepted to America!

Very early the next morning Mirjana woke to a slight movement on her pillow. She saw a bright orange resting there. A guard waved at her as he walked away in silence with a smile.

Hours later, the Croatian family left the USS General Hersey with the shadow of Lady Liberty on their shoulders. The land of opportunity belonged to them.

They considered it a blessing – a sponsor from a small town in Ohio had agreed to take the entire family without splitting them apart. The sponsor family wanted to help the victims of war.

With these heroic thoughts in their minds, Anton hurried his family onto a train that chugged out of New York City to its destination in Ohio.

Katica's hand brushed against the name tag pinned on her sweater. She looked at her family. The predominate name tags fastened to their clothes told who they were and where they were going.

Darkness overtook the train. Its rolling, heavy wheels would take them through the entire night to Ohio.

Hannah and Matej, Katica and Anton processed every aspect of their new surroundings. At the same time, Mirjana and Maria felt apprehension and great interest.

An American soldier walked down the train aisle. For a moment he hesitated and then stopped by Mirjana and Maria's seat. They looked at him without saying a word.

The soldier placed his hand in his pocket and pulled out two candy bars. He was pleased to give the candy to the girls. Mirjana said, "Thank you, Sir" with English words she learned in the Austrian school.

Hours later, the train raced on when a fear overtook the girls. A suspicious man stood before them. Mirjana and Maria were more afraid than Katica and Hannah. They were not used to seeing a man of color. It would be very unusual in Croatia. With kindness he gave a grapefruit and a banana to them. This was a pleasant surprise by another American.

A concern for Anton and Matej was the lack of money. They had none. The only food they had eaten was a boxed chicken dinner provided on the train. Their stomachs grumbled in protest as the train thundered along the rails.

Once again morning came on this long journey to freedom. They had never heard a bad word about America. At last, a train conductor bellowed out, "Next stop for your destination, be ready please."

They grabbed their small bags and moved towards the door of the train. With a jolt, the train ground to a complete stop. The family stayed close to each other after they stepped off the train.

Within minutes a man, their sponsor, rushed to them. "Welcome, welcome to America and your new home."

Robert, their American sponsor, smiled as he opened his car doors for them. The family climbed in with contentment on their faces and eyes open wide.

"I hope you are not too crowded," Robert said, as he glanced around at them.

Mirjana was quick to answer, "We are just so glad to be here." In her thoughts, she could not believe that at sixteen years of age, she would be beginning a new life in the United States of America. Mirjana felt pure joy!

Robert spoke again. "We have so much to talk about. I own a custom tailoring firm and I need a tailor."

Anton was proud to answer, "I am ready to serve you. My tailoring skills were known to be of high quality in Croatia."

With sincere interest Robert replied, "I understand you also worked on military uniforms."

"Yes, I did. It was not my favorite work but necessary," Anton responded.

Mirjana's ability with the English language enabled them all to communicate with their new American friends.

****

The calm, peaceful days of life in America began. From the years of 1951 to 1953, the family lived with their sponsor, Robert, and his family.

Anton worked with enthusiasm and pride as a tailor for Robert's firm. Katica cleaned the house that became a real home for them all. Mirjana and Maria attended school, learned the language and practiced vocabulary after school. They adjusted to their new life with memories tucked away in their hearts.

When Mirjana became eighteen years old, change found its way into their pleasant lives. Anton gathered his family together and told them the news, "We are moving to upstate New York to a village named Georgiana."

Mirjana and Maria looked at their mother to see her reaction. They watched as Katica's eyes filled with tears. Katica's lips trembled as she spoke, "We have found other family members who have lived there since 1951 with their sponsor from the local church."

It was time for both sponsors to give up their responsibility of their refugees. Once again the family from Croatia packed their belongings to move. When the last "thank you" was spoken and the last hug given, they packed themselves into an old station wagon car.

Katica's emotional words poured out, "It is wise and good to remember what an impact we can have on other people's lives. Extraordinary! It doesn't happen everyday." Mirjana and Maria allowed their mother's words to slip deep within them.

****

Many days later, they arrived in Georgiana, New York.

The roughness of history, the roughness of life had passed. A Croatian family was reunited!

Anton and Matej had saved money from their work in Ohio. They purchased a small home together. They soon discovered other Croatian families living in and around their new town.

One sunny afternoon, the church held a picnic on its back lawn. The soft, green grass was fringed with lavender lilac bushes. Mirjana and Maria watched as all the ladies placed large dishes and bowls on the picnic tables. American and Croatian food rested side by side waiting to be devoured.

The young children raced and played together. Mirjana and Maria looked on as it happened.

"Maria, that man near the maple tree; he looks familiar," Mirjana said to her sister.

"The one walking away? I only had a glimpse of him," Maria answered.

"I think he lived close to us in Croatia. Come with me, Maria. We need to find him," Mirjana said as she coaxed her sister to follow her.

They walked among the people, exchanged pleasant words and watched for the man from Croatia. "I can't wait to try all that food," said Maria. "You go ahead and try to find him."

It was important for Mirjana to connect with someone from her long-ago home. She tipped her head to smell the natural perfume of a lilac blossom. Near the end of the large, beautiful bush stood the man she was looking for. "Hello, are you from Croatia?" Mirjana asked.

"Yes, you look familiar to me also. We lived in the same small village near the church, didn't we?" he answered as he stared at Mirjana with interest. "My name is Jakov."

"Oh, yes, I remember, you played the button game in the dirt with the other guys," Mirjana continued.

"We each had a bag filled with the colorful buttons we won. A string held the bag closed," Jakov spoke with a sigh. Each word brought back a pleasant memory before the horrors of war.

"I always wondered where you boys got all those buttons to toss along the ground," Mirjana asked.

He answered with a twinkle in his eye, "We snipped them off people's clothing." Mirjana smiled as she watched the orange sun slip towards the horizon.

"I think we should exchange addresses and write to each other," Jakov said.

Mirjana tried to hide her thoughts: a handsome man from Croatia with dark hair and kind eyes wants to write to her. Mirjana searched her bag for a pencil and paper. She found them, wrote her information, and Jakov did the same.

The soft touch of his hand with the deep, direct look into her eyes gave Mirjana a message without words. Their letters would be swift and frequent.

They shared a history of a country under the dark cloud of war. The violence of war and the specter of death always present had forced both families to leave their homeland.

****

After many years in a different place, in a different time, they found each other. The process of letter writing grew into love.

An old acquaintance in a new land, love became marriage. Mirjana experienced all that was possible, all she had hoped for.

The passage of time brought children and successful careers and yet there was a restlessness in Mirjana. She could not explain it but the pull was intense. Mirjana felt a strong desire to return to the country of her birth, Croatia.

CHAPTER 17

THE RETURN TO CROATIA

The time in America passed from one tranquil year to the next. Deep sorrow was only experienced when Grandmother Hannah and Grandfather Matej passed from this life.

One evening after dinner, Anton and Katica sat together on the deep, soft cushions of their favorite furniture. Katica took Anton's hands into her own and rubbed his strong hands with gentle motions. "Anton, I'd like to talk with you for awhile," she said.

"Of course Katica, go on. We have a quiet evening ahead," Anton answered.

"You know our life in America has been so good. We have come so far from the thin children of confinement camps and war," Katica began.

"I can still see how thin we were, like skin pulled and stretched over our bones," Anton said as he remembered.

"Here in America we have delicious food and work. We feel we can contribute to this great country we now live in and we have our independence too," Katica spoke her thoughts out loud.

Anton said with strong words, almost fierce in tone, "The United States of America granted us citizenship, a noble reward for being part of this country. We will continue to make America proud of us."

"Oh yes, citizenship, a gift we did not know in Europe," Katica responded. "There is one more thing. It's about Mirjana. She has an immense longing to return to Croatia."

With a quick reply Anton said, "We must let her go, even encourage her."

"Of course, we'll talk to her soon," Katica said with her eyes in a far-away place.

Within two days, Anton, Katica, Mirjana and Maria had the talk. Travel plans were made and the plane ticket was purchased. Mirjana made arrangements to travel with her cousin who lived nearby.

****

On the day of their departure from the huge New York City airport, Mirjana pulled her carry-on bag in one hand and clutched her boarding pass with her other. After passing through the gate to their plane, she turned one more time. Mirjana looked at her aging parents and her younger sister, Maria. Her gaze lingered longer on her husband, Jakov. With a faint smile, she waved good-bye.

The time on the large, silver plane crept by hour after

hour. Mirjana and her cousin, Elisabeth, slept a little and talked often. They were about the same age and shared many common memories. Mirjana asked Elisabeth, "Do you remember the dandelion fields?"

Elisabeth answered, "Yes, we walked among those yellow flowers and picked their leaves."

Mirjana nodded in agreement. "I can still taste those dandelion greens salads. We ate so many."

Elisabeth added, "Sometime, someone from the Red Cross took a photo of us."

Their conversation ended with the descent of the plane and the landing with a smooth heavy thud on the runway. As Mirjana disembarked from the plane, the entire scope of her trip filled every fiber of her body. She said to herself with silent words, "You are standing where you stood as a child." She felt more memories flood back.

Now, more than a half a century later, Mirjana returned to the capital city of Croatia. She visited museums and historic sites. With sadness she saw the bullet holes in buildings. Mirjana remembered the machine guns from the low-flying planes. Their rapid-striking bullets made those holes.

Mirjana walked farther to find only the church entrance still stood in its place. The bombs had destroyed her entire church. Her sorrow deepened as she found the cemetery where many family members were buried. As she walked, Mirjana stepped with care over cracked stone graves. Some granite family memorials had been smashed into small fragments. War had desecrated the resting place of many loved ones.

Mirjana's eyes filled with large tears. She reached into her pocket for a colorful handkerchief. Mirjana was prepared, she feared she would need one. She dried her eyes and continued the poignant journey into the past.

Mirjana's walk brought her to the National Archives Building. Curiosity bubbled inside her as she walked through the entrance.

Mirjana's eyes absorbed the exquisite beauty of the interior. Elaborate carved wood moldings outlined the walls and ceilings. Paint tinted with tiny specks of gold covered the walls. The delicate yet intense surroundings heightened Mirjana's desire to know more of the past.

The curator approached her and asked, "How may I help you?"

"Tell me what the archives are," Mirjana answered.

The woman curator replied, "Are you Croatian? Were you born here?"

"Yes, yes again," responded Mirjana with an inquisitive tone.

The curator retrieved the town files and the year of Mirjana's birth. With kind words she showed Mirjana how to use the files.

Many names filled page after page of the records. She was amazed at the large number of names she recognized.

Mirjana searched for her mother and father's names. Her entire body became still as she stared at the worn yet clear page. Mirjana found their names. Her eyes did not blink as she read Katica, Anton and the date of their marriage.

Without warning, a sharp pain pierced her heart and

churned her stomach. Mirjana's legs felt weak. There had been a baby girl with no name. The baby was very small, very beautiful and death overtook her. A short note in parenthesis stated "red hair." Mirjana knew Croatians did not have red hair. Their hair was shades of brown or black.

Mirjana's shock increased as she read the black ink words. The mother's name was Katica! The father was unknown!

She tried to subdue her intense emotions and called the curator. "Tell me why the father's name was not listed for the baby who did not live." Mirjana's words almost broke apart in the air as she spoke.

The curator explained with gentleness, "Often, if the father was nobility, his name was not listed. A mother would remain quiet to prevent shame or embarrassment to the noble father."

Mirjana could not deny the written words as they stood out with truth and boldness on the old page before her eyes.

Mirjana continued to read. She found her name, Maria's name and her parents' names, Katica and Anton, again as in the lines before. The birth dates of Mirjana and Maria were correct.

Stunned in heart and soul, Mirjana left the Archive Building. Who is she? A large part of her identity had been locked away in Croatian history.

Had the blood of royalty mingled with the common blood of peasants? It had happened before in a large Manor House with towers.

In a mental cloud of colored emotions, Mirjana remembered stories of secret meetings in large, old barns. Behind closed, heavy barn doors, couples met. A trusted family member stood in place just outside the barn. A bright lantern was held in their hand as a signal.

A beloved aunt had told the true stories to Mirjana. She gave little thought to her aunt's words until now. Could a Baron or a Baron's son have met a special girl in a secret spot?

****

The plane ride back to America was a blur of facts held captive by Katica's secret. As their return flight landed in the bustling New York City airport, Mirjana wanted to rush from the plane to see her family.

At last all her baggage was found as her eyes searched for Jakov, Katica, Anton and Maria. Mirjana approached the Customs Officer who was her last hurtle to re-enter the United States. He checked her passport and papers. With a loud voice he said, "Welcome Home, Mirjana!"

The Customs Officer did not know the importance of his words. She would never forget his warm voice and welcome greeting. Deep inside, Mirjana felt "yes", this is my home.

Jakov saw her first. He and her parents and sister all raced to each other and enjoyed extra long embraces. It would be a new beginning for them all where the past blended with the present and truth with love grew together.

Katica looked at Anton, with tears blurring her vision, she said, "Mirjana knows."

****

In the sometimes fiery, sometimes delicate nature of human relationships, feelings may be expressed or buried. During times of war, the mind reacts with a depth of horror and creative survival. The tenacity of the human spirit for survival can never be denied.

The tarnished secrets they brought with them were polished by experiences until they glowed with their new lives.

ACKNOWLEDGEMENTS

My pages of handwritten words transformed into a manuscript with the computer talent and knowledge of two remarkable women. Joanne DePauw, a close friend of 50 years and Francine Bremer, a sister-in-law who is more like a sister, are the reason for the completion of this book. I give them my deepest gratitude.

There are other friends and family who supported my writing. In their humility they chose not to be mentioned. They still deserve a thank you.

Like a fuzzy caterpillar becomes a stunning butterfly, my humble sentences grew into this book.

Made in the USA
Middletown, DE
01 November 2020